The Veteran's Holiday Home

Lee Tobin McClain

Recycling programs for this product may not exist in your area.

ISBN-13: 978-1-335-58526-4

The Veteran's Holiday Home

Love Inspired
22 Adelaide St. West, 41st Floor
Toronto, Ontario M5H 4E3, Canada
www.LoveInspired.com

Printed in U.S.A.

"I didn't realize the two of you knew each other..."

"The website didn't have a picture—" Jason began.

"You always went by Jason in the family—" Ashley said at the same time.

They both laughed awkwardly.

"You really didn't know it was me who'd be interviewing you?" she asked, her voice skeptical.

If he'd known the job would involve working with his late half brother's wife, he'd never have applied. Ashley presented a different kind of risk.

Being constantly reminded of his brilliant, successful younger brother, the difficulties of his home life... No. He'd escaped all that, and no way was he going back.

His own feelings for his brother's wife notwithstanding. He'd felt sorry for her, had tried to help, but she'd spurned his help and pushed him away.

And getting involved with her was a mistake he wouldn't make again.

But *this* was what he needed if he was going to heal and thrive. Just beautiful views and the chance to make a difference.

He hadn't reckoned on having Ashley for a boss, though.

This changed everything...

Lee Tobin McClain is the *New York Times* bestselling author of emotional small-town romances featuring flawed characters who find healing through friendship, faith and family. Lee grew up in Ohio and now lives in Western Pennsylvania, where she enjoys hiking with her goofy goldendoodle, visiting writer friends and admiring her daughter's mastery of the latest TikTok dances. Learn more about her books at www.leetobinmcclain.com.

Books by Lee Tobin McClain

Love Inspired

K-9 Companions

Her Easter Prayer
The Veteran's Holiday Home

Rescue Haven

The Secret Christmas Child
Child on His Doorstep
Finding a Christmas Home

Redemption Ranch

The Soldier's Redemption
The Twins' Family Christmas
The Nanny's Secret Baby

Visit the Author Profile page at LoveInspired.com for more titles.

For thou, Lord, art good, and ready to forgive;
and plenteous in mercy unto all them
that call upon thee.

—*Psalm* 86:5

To My Readers

Chapter One

Principal Ashley Green looked at the redheaded, freckle-faced eleven-year-old in front of her and tried to maintain a stern expression.

Working with students was her favorite part of her job at Bright Tomorrows Residential Academy.

Her next favorite part might be the view out her office window. The gorgeous Colorado Rocky Mountains always offered perspective, even on a cold, snowy November day.

She refocused on the boy squirming in the hard wooden chair in front of her desk—the hot seat, as the students called it.

"You're going to have to help Ms. Ferguson clean up the science classroom after school all this week," she said. "And that's in addition to helping her clean up the mess you caused when you mixed chemicals to make an explosion. That could have been dangerous." It hadn't been, not really. The younger kids were well supervised, their access to anything hazardous limited.

But if Ricky continued disobeying the rules in science class, he'd get to the point where he could do some real damage.

"It was so cool, though! You should have seen it, Dr. Green!"

She lifted an eyebrow at him and managed not to smile. "Believe me, I got a full report from Ms. Ferguson. The word *cool* wasn't used."

His face fell. "I'm sorry. I shoulda thought before I acted."

He was so cute, parroting the scolding he'd no doubt received dozens of times. He really didn't mean any harm. Still, every boy at the academy was here due to discipline problems at other schools and, usually, at home as well. It was crucial that they turn their lives around. For some of them, Bright Tomorrows was their last chance.

Thinking of last chances reminded her of her discussion with the board of trustees two days ago. The school was in financial trouble, and if they didn't fix it by increasing enrollment, there was a possibility they'd have to close their doors at the end of the school year.

That was unacceptable. She had a personal stake in helping these boys learn to distinguish right from wrong.

As Ricky gathered up his things, Ashley thought ahead to the next item on her to-do list. She hoped to hire a new industrial arts teacher, since her current one had just given notice. In two weeks, she'd have a roomful of boys—including Ricky—without a teacher. Shop class wasn't something the rest of her staff could pinch-hit on. She was interviewing the one and only applicant this morning and praying that he'd be a qualified, competent teacher.

"Okay, Ricky, head back to class, and no more trouble, please."

Ricky hurried out, his crutches and the cast on his leg—a result of yet another act of mischief gone wrong—making his gait awkward. At the doorway, he turned back. "See ya, Dr. Green," he yelled with a bright, friendly smile that warmed Ashley's heart. She really did love these kids.

"Careful, honey," called Mrs. Henry, the school secretary.

But the warning came too late. Ricky crashed into a giant dog and reeled back.

Ashley scrambled out from behind her desk and rushed toward the teetering boy. A fall couldn't be good for his complex fracture. How had a dog, a terrifying one like that, gotten into the school?

She wasn't going to make it in time.

Beside the dog and half out of sight, a big man reached down and grabbed Ricky by the waist, lifting him up and swinging him to the side, away from the creature.

The man's own cane clattered to the floor.

He set Ricky on his feet, making sure he was steady on his crutches and well away from the dog. And then—oh no—he started to stumble himself.

The dog moved directly into his path and he grabbed at its harness and caught himself, wincing, his other hand going to his back. He turned to Ricky, who still looked terrified. "You're okay," he said, his voice strained but gentle. "He's a good dog, my helper. Do you want to visit with him?"

That voice. So familiar.

Ricky hesitated, then nodded.

"Go say hi," the man said to the dog, his voice subtly shifting into a sterner tone that showed he was giving the animal a command. He was holding on to the doorjamb for balance, his body stiff and a little hunched.

The dog looked up at the man and then down at the cane on the ground.

The man chuckled. "Okay, Titan, you're right. Pick up the cane."

The dog picked up the cane with his mouth and handed it to the man. Then he walked over to Ricky, tail wagging, and stood while the boy tentatively patted his big head.

Ashley stared at the man, her heart rate going up, up, up.

He looked the same and yet totally different.

She wanted to run far away from the memories he evoked, memories of the worst time in her life. But she was the leader here and had to fulfill her responsibilities. She forced herself to take a few steps toward Ricky, the big man and the dog. "You should get to class, Ricky," she said.

The boy seemed about to argue, but he took one look at her face and nodded. "See ya, Dr. Green. Thanks, mister." He limped out of the office and headed down the hall.

Mrs. Henry bustled over to the man and dog. "Come on in. You must be Mr. Smith, here for the interview, am I right? And you've already gotten a taste of the urchins who go to school here. I'm sorry Ricky ran into you. Can I get you a cup of coffee?"

Ashley took deep breaths, trying to compose herself as the past flooded back into her mind. Most notably, the time this man had saved *her*. And rather than thanking him as Ricky had, she'd pushed him away, made him question what he'd seen. Basically, lied to him.

Now she backed slowly into her office. Jason didn't seem to have noticed her yet. She fumbled behind her, never taking her eyes off him, and reached for his résumé, which had been printed out and sitting on her desk.

She found it, atop copies of his clearances and a couple of strong recommendation letters. She'd actually been excited about this candidate. How could this have happened, that she'd seen no hint of who he really was?

She looked at the front of the résumé. J. C. Smith.

Otherwise known as Jason Smith, her late husband's brother.

Jason stared at the woman in the doorway of the principal's office. "*You're* A. Green?"

Just looking at her sent shock waves through him. What had happened to his late brother's wife?

She was still gorgeous, no doubt. But she was much thinner than she'd been when he'd last seen her, her strong cheekbones standing out above full lips, still pretty, although now without benefit of lipstick. She wore a business suit, the blouse underneath buttoned up to her chin.

Her eyes still had that vulnerable look in them, though, the one that had sucked him into making a mistake, doing what he shouldn't have done. Making a phone call with disastrous results.

She recovered before he did. "Come in. You'll want to sit down," she said. "I'm sorry about Ricky running into you and your dog."

He followed her into her office.

"Have a seat," she said, gesturing toward a chair.

He waited for her to sit down behind her desk before easing himself into it. He wasn't supposed to lift anything above fifty pounds and he wasn't supposed to twist, and the way his back felt right now, after doing both, proved his orthopedic doctor was right. Pain radiated from his spine out through his arms and up into his neck, and he shifted back and forth, trying to find a comfortable position.

Beside him, Titan whined and moved closer, and Jason put a hand on the big dog. "Lie down," he ordered, but gently. Titan had saved him from a bad fall.

"I didn't realize the two of you knew each other," the secretary said. "Can I get you both some coffee?"

"We're fine," Ashley said, and even though Jason had been about to decline the offer, he looked a question at her. Was she too hostile to even give a man a beverage?

The older woman backed out of the office. The door clicked shut.

Leaving Ashley and Jason alone.

"The website didn't have a picture—" he began.

"You always went by Jason in the family—" she said at the same time.

They both laughed, awkwardly.

"You really didn't know it was me who'd be interviewing you?" she asked, her voice skeptical.

"No. Your website's kind of…limited." He was trying to be tactful, but the thing was pathetic.

If he'd known the job would involve working with his late half brother's wife, he'd never have applied. Too many bad memories, and while he'd been fortunate to come out of the combat zone with fewer mental health issues than some vets, he had to watch his frame of mind, take care about the kind of environment he lived in.

That was one reason he'd liked the looks of this job, high in the Colorado Rocky Mountains. He needed to get out of the risky neighborhood where he was living.

Ashley presented a different kind of risk.

Being constantly reminded of his brilliant, successful younger brother, so much more suave and popular and talented than Jason was, at least on the outside… being reminded of the difficulties of his home life after his mom had married Christopher's dad…no. He'd escaped all that, and no way was he going back.

His own feelings for his brother's wife notwithstanding. He'd felt sorry for her, had tried to help, but she'd spurned his help and pushed him away.

Getting involved with her was a mistake he wouldn't make again.

"I…I'm so surprised to see you," she said, her voice faint. "Let alone to have you come here to interview for a job. I'd never have guessed it."

"Doesn't help that Smith is such a common name. I get it." He and Christopher didn't even have the same last name; once his mom had remarried, he'd been the only Smith in the family. Just one of the many ways he didn't fit in with the rest of them.

And now here he was with Christopher's wife, and she was looking at him with a sort of disbelief. That might have to do with his obvious disability and the tattoos that were visible on his wrists, but more likely had to do with the past.

He looked around her office to give her time to recover. Himself, too.

The place didn't give him much of a clue into who

she was as a person. An old-fashioned metal file cabinet, a battered desk and a couple of shelves full of books that looked like textbooks. Another shelf of notebooks. No wall decor. Looked like Ashley was all business, these days.

Only the window facing out onto a mountain view added beauty, but that more than made up for the plainness. Jutting snowcapped peaks were barely visible thanks to a fog of clouds, the sun glowing behind them, about to burst through. Closer in, foothills were covered with dark pines interspersed with a few aspens still holding their golden leaves.

This was what he needed if he was going to heal and thrive. No city noises here; no dealers next door hawking their tempting wares. Just beautiful views and the chance to make a difference. As he'd driven up the lonely road to the school, he'd gotten happier and happier about the possibility of working at a place tucked away into the rugged, natural beauty of the Rocky Mountains.

He hadn't reckoned with having Ashley for a boss, though. That changed everything. Should he tell her it just wouldn't work, turn around, walk away?

From the job that, otherwise, seemed like a God-given opportunity tailor-made for him?

It wasn't as if there were a lot of choices for a man with no paid experience in his new field. Plus a disability that would cause some employers to reject him for made-up reasons just because it made them uncomfortable.

He made the only logical decision. "I'd still like to interview for the job, if it's okay with you," he said.

Her eyes reflected panic, but she picked up a couple

of pages from her desk. His résumé. "Of course. Let's talk about your experience, since it looks like this would be your first teaching job."

That made him sound like a kid, and at thirty-five, he was anything but. "I had a rough stretch when I came back from overseas," he said, as his VA adviser had coached. *Be honest, but don't overshare.* "It took two years to finish the degree I started online while I was in the service. I did my student teaching last year, at a school for juvenile offenders."

Her face clouded. "That's exactly where I want to prevent these boys from going," she said.

"Excellent plan. Juvie isn't the greatest place for a kid." He paused. "I met a lot of people from all different backgrounds during my time overseas. I liked working with the ones who'd had a rough road as kids." No need to tell her that he identified, because he'd been such an underdog in his own family. "That's why I wanted to work with young offenders in my student teaching, and that's why Bright Tomorrows sounds like my kind of place."

"That's good. It's important our teachers get behind our mission." She still looked skeptical.

He cleared his throat and went into the next explanation he'd practiced. "I'm sure you can tell that I have some mobility issues—"

She held up a hand. "No need to explain. We can make accommodations if you're hired."

Good, she was ADA compliant, but he didn't like that "if." He wanted this job, badly. Or at least he had until he'd realized he was likely to be working with Ashley Green.

But maybe not too closely, so he should go for it and

make a decision later, after—*if*—he got an offer. "I don't always use a cane," he explained, "but I almost always have Titan with me."

The mastiff lifted his head at the sound of his name.

"He's a fully certified service dog, and well trained, so he shouldn't be disruptive."

"Our reading teacher has a service dog as well," she said. "Although…not such a big one." She looked doubtfully at Titan, and Jason had a vague memory of Christopher telling him she'd had a bad experience with a dog when she was small.

"I can do everything needed in an industrial arts class," he continued, leaning forward a little, trying not to reveal how the movement hurt. "Except if there's something heavy to be lifted. I may need some help with that."

She raised an eyebrow. "Something heavy, like an eleven-year-old boy who crashed into your dog?"

"Yeah." He sat back and the change of position made him wince. "That was instinct on my part. Titan would never have hurt the child, but he looked like he was losing his balance with that cast."

She nodded. "Thank you for helping him at the expense of your own comfort." She paused. "And thank you for what you did for our country. I'm sorry for what you've gone through."

Her words sounded sincere, unlike some platitudes he'd heard, and he appreciated that.

Still, she wasn't diving into interview questions, which made him suspect he'd lost his chance for this job. He should have done as his VA adviser said and used his connections to a couple of the school's board members, but he'd wanted to get the job on his own.

Typical. He'd always been independent, sometimes to the point of stupidity.

This was one of those instances, because if he didn't get this job, what was he going to do? He knew well enough the risks of staying where he'd been living before. The place he could afford in Denver was in a rough neighborhood, and when his pain got bad, he had only to walk to the street corner for the opioids that could make it all go away.

He refused to turn into someone who let chronic pain ruin his life. He couldn't serve his country anymore, not like he had in the past, but he wanted to make a difference, and this job had sounded perfect.

Was perfect, except that his boss would be Ashley, his half brother's wife. Ashley, who'd begged him to stay away from her.

If she still felt that way, there was no point. He wouldn't grovel. "Look," he said, "is this even a possibility? Because if you're set against hiring me, I'll take off."

She looked down at her desk for a moment, then met his eyes. "I'm not going to lie," she said. "It would be difficult, given our past history. Your parents despise me and I'm completely out of their lives."

"I'm not that close with them myself." She'd changed from the woman she'd been, under his brother's thumb. She seemed…stronger.

"Are *you* still interested, given that you'd be working with me?" she asked bluntly.

"How closely?" he asked.

"I mean, we're a small school. But I have a lot of teachers to supervise, a lot of budgeting and paperwork to take care of. And students to handle." She gestured in the direction the kid with the cast had gone, one corner of her mouth turning up in something like a smile. "For example, Ricky, who created an explosion in his science class."

Jason couldn't restrain a chuckle. "Was that before or after he broke his leg?"

"After. The leg was from when he climbed on top of one of our outbuildings and fell off. So you see what you'd be dealing with." Her smile widened, revealing that single dimple that had always made her look so cute.

Now it moderated the severity of her clothes and pulled-back hair, reminding him of the girl she'd been.

And he was losing focus. He grasped for what she'd said. "In other words, we'd both be busy with kids like Ricky and we wouldn't be working together that closely."

"Correct." She went into an explanation of the class schedule, the responsibilities, the perks. "Normally we have housing for our teachers, if they want it, but our cabins are all occupied right now."

Too bad. That had been an appealing part of the job description. "If you're not turning me down flat, I'm not turning you down flat," he said.

"We should both take a little time to think about it." She bit her lip. "I only have a couple of weeks to make this hire, though, so we'll need to think fast. Meanwhile, I'll give you our usual tour of the facilities and grounds, if you'd like." She glanced at Titan and then at him. "We could skip the tour or arrange another time if that would work better."

He appreciated that she was checking in about his ability to walk around and doing it without being patronizing. "I'd like to see the place."

"Let's head out, then." She stood.

He tried to stand, too, but his back seized up. "Stand," he said to Titan, and then, "Stay." He grasped the rigid handle of Titan's harness and pulled himself to his feet. "Let's go," he said, and they followed Ashley to the door.

She waited and walked through the outside door, holding it for him and Titan. The sun lit up her gold hair, neatly tied back but with a few strands escaping.

She was still gorgeous, and he still felt the same tug toward her that he'd felt years ago. But he ignored it. Even if she hadn't been his brother's wife, she would have been off-limits to a big, not-so-bright, not-so-successful man like him. He couldn't let that bother him.

That would be the least of his problems if he got—and took—this job.

Chapter Two

As they walked across the school grounds, Ashley tried not to be obvious about the fact that she was studying the man beside her.

Jason had always been a big man, much bigger than his half brother, Christopher, her husband. Even with the slightly hunched way he walked now, he was well over six feet tall. And he was even more muscular than the last time she'd seen him. No wonder he needed such a big service dog.

"How long have you had Titan?" she asked, just to make conversation.

"For the past year." He glanced down at the dog, buff-colored with a darker face and ears. "He's a big help. And completely gentle, if you're concerned about the kids."

She nodded. The dog was obviously well trained, but his head was huge, which meant his teeth would be as well. She shivered involuntarily.

"I remember Christopher saying you'd been bitten in childhood," Jason said.

Even hearing Christopher's name made her insides twist uncomfortably. "I'm mostly over that."

"Look, should we talk about what happened between us before? Because—"

"No." She put up a hand, waved it to stop him talking. Her heart pounded uncomfortably. She was being cowardly, but thinking about Christopher and the past might make her fall apart, and she couldn't do that at work. "I'm not sure this is going to work."

He blew out a sigh. "Maybe you're right."

And maybe she was being selfish and unfair, but she just didn't think she could do it.

She turned toward the parking lot and he followed her, the path taking them by her place. She looked longingly at the big, sprawling farmhouse, now divided into a duplex. She'd love to go inside, turn on the gas fire and curl up with an escapist book.

"Ashley!" The door to the other side of the duplex opened, and Matt McConner, the industrial arts teacher who was leaving, came out, waving her down. He strode over, nodded at Jason and put a hand on her arm. "The doctor called and she's concerned about something in Missy's blood work. She wants us closer to the specialists at the hospital there." He paused. "I hate to do this to you, but we're going to have to move down to Denver right away. I've been calling around to try to find us a sub, but so far—"

He was sweating, his forehead wrinkled in concern, and he kept glancing back at the house. No doubt his pregnant wife, Missy, was there.

Missy's health trumped any other problems. "Don't worry about finding a sub. That's my job. You take care of Missy."

His expression relaxed a little, but he still frowned. "I gave you a month's notice. I feel awful about leaving before that's over."

"Forget about that," Ashley said. "What can I do to help?" Matt and Missy had been her duplex mates since the summer, and they'd quickly become friends, were constantly in and out of each other's homes. She knew how long they'd been trying to conceive and how excited they were about their baby. If something was wrong…

Missy, visibly pregnant—she was about six months along—came out onto the porch. She held up her phone. "My brother says he can bring his truck up tomorrow to get our stuff," she called to Matt. She leaned on the railing and looked down at Ashley. "I'm so sorry. I know this puts you in a tough spot."

Ashley hurried up the porch steps and hugged her friend. "Don't give it another thought. Just stay well. Are you doing okay?" She stepped back and studied Missy's face.

"I'm scared," Missy admitted, "but we've been praying throughout the whole pregnancy and we still are. It's in God's hands."

"I'll pray for you, too." Just like every time she promised to pray, Ashley shot up a quick prayer immediately. "I'm going to miss you! You have to keep me posted on everything."

Missy looked behind Ashley. "Who's *that*?"

Ashley glanced back and realized that Jason still stood on the sidelines, waiting for her to be finished with her conversation. Titan stood beside him. And was Jason leaning on the dog a little?

Yikes. For a minute, she'd forgotten about him. She shouldn't have left him standing there.

"He's…a guy I'm interviewing," Ashley said. "For Matt's job, actually."

"He's a beast! You're sure he's not a gang lord or something?" Missy said and then clapped her hand over her mouth. "I'm sorry. I shouldn't stereotype. I just mean he's…big."

"Well, his *dog* is a beast, for sure." Ashley studied man and dog. Jason had always been big, and rugged, but his face seemed squarer now, his shoulders more solid. His dark hair was cut short, suggesting his military background.

"Do you think you'll hire him?"

"Not sure yet." And for the first time, her situation sank in. Her industrial arts teacher was leaving, not in a month as she'd thought, but today.

Her phone buzzed, and when she looked down, she realized it was the chairman of Bright Tomorrows' board of directors. Her boss. "Sorry, I have to take this," she said to Missy, and gave an apologetic wave to Jason, who nodded his understanding.

"I hear from your secretary that our candidate came up on his own." Thomas Wilkins was called the Captain for more reasons than one. That was the rank at which he'd retired from the Marine Corps, and that was his leadership style.

"Who's your candidate?" she asked, although she had a sinking feeling that she knew.

"Jason Smith. Decorated combat vet. He can start that military program I've been trying to get you to implement. You're hiring him, right?"

Ashley's hackles rose as she paced away from Missy

and Jason, seeking more privacy for the conversation. She looked up at the mountains. *Lord, grant me patience.* "Captain Wilkins, I obviously take your opinions seriously, but as the principal—"

"As principal, you need to keep Bright Tomorrows in business," he said in a bullying tone. "According to Admissions, the number one question parents have about the school is the postsecondary transition and placement rate. Ours is weak."

Ashley sucked in a breath and let it out slowly. The Captain wasn't wrong. "We've increased the percentage of students who go on for postsecondary education—"

"But it's still low, and our job placement isn't good. Which is why we need to encourage a stint in the military. Today's young people are lazy. They don't want to work hard. The idea of military service doesn't appeal the way it did to my generation."

Ashley refrained from reminding him about the complicated history of the military and the draft during the Vietnam era, when he had come of age. He knew it, of course, but when he was on a rant, he conveniently forgot.

"They need to be exposed to the armed services throughout school," he continued, "so they see it as a desirable option. Jason Smith is the man who can help you develop the program."

Ashley kept her eyes focused on the mountains, trying to sort through her options as she listened to Thomas with half an ear. She really didn't *have* options. Not with Matt leaving this very afternoon.

Finding qualified teachers who wanted to live here, or in the tiny nearby town of Little Mesa, wasn't easy. Even those who were willing to live locally often preferred to work in the public school system, with its higher pay and less troubled kids.

You had to have a heart for the Bright Tomorrows mission of helping troubled boys. Had to see past their acting out and look at the promising young men underneath. From what he'd said, Jason had that.

If she didn't know him, didn't have a history with him, he'd seem like the perfect candidate for the job.

But she *did* know him, did have a history with him. He knew too much about her past.

"All of our on-site cabins are occupied," she said when the Captain took a breath.

"Where did the teacher who's leaving stay?" he asked.

She paused. "In the other half of the duplex where I live," she admitted.

"Well, there you go."

Ashley's stomach churned. No. No way. She could *not* both work with Jason and live next door to him. "I don't think that's going to work."

"Don't think. Hire the guy." The Captain hung up on her.

She swallowed. Shoved her phone in her pocket. Took one more look at the distant mountain peaks. She closed her eyes, shot up a prayer for guidance and then turned back toward Jason.

Missy had gone inside. Matt was carrying suitcases to their SUV.

Jason stood, his arms crossed, looking at her. It was as if he knew she'd been talking about him. As if, she thought as she slowly, reluctantly, walked closer, he could see into her soul.

She stopped in front of him. Looked directly back

into those penetrating eyes and straightened her shoulders. "If you want the job," she said with a sinking feeling, "it's yours."

Later that evening, Jason was still reeling from the fact that he'd received a job offer from Ashley Green.

A job offer.

From a woman he'd never expected to see again in his life. And for whom he had extremely complicated feelings.

"We can walk over to my friends' house for dinner, or drive." Jason's host for the night, Pastor Nate Fisher, locked the front door of his small home in Little Mesa, the town nearest Bright Tomorrows, and turned to Jason. "Have a preference? It's just on the other side of downtown. A ten-minute walk or a two-minute drive."

Jason rubbed Titan's head. "This guy would love a walk, and it would be good for me, too," he said.

They headed for the street and turned left toward Little Mesa's tiny downtown, Titan ambling beside them. The sun was setting behind the peaks to the west, making the clouds glow in pink and gold bands. The chilly air smelled fresh, like pine trees and sage.

"Sorry I'm not cooking for you," Nate said, "but we'll be a lot better off eating at Dev and Emily McCarthy's place. I'm strictly an 'open a can of soup' kind of guy."

"I'm just grateful that you're putting me up," Jason said truthfully. One of his faculty mentors, the one who'd told him about the job at Bright Tomorrows, knew Nate and had asked if Jason could stay the night after interviewing for the job.

"You may not be so grateful when you've slept on my

pullout couch." Nate looked over at him. "If you sleep diagonally, I guess you can fit, but as for comfort…"

"Hey, it's easier on my wallet than trying to find a hotel. And it beats driving back to Denver tonight." Jason had to accept his own limits. After a stressful day, fatigue was a problem. He couldn't drive all night the way he had as a younger man, before a mortar shell had filled his spine with shrapnel.

They were walking through the downtown now, passing a hardware store that was still open and a bakery that was closed. A few trucks drove past, one driver honking and waving at Nate. There were pedestrians on the sidewalks, a mother with two kids, a small group of teenagers, and several older couples, one of whom was walking a chubby basset hound who gave a single low woof as it passed Titan.

Titan's head turned to watch the dog as it lumbered past, but he stayed at Jason's side.

"He's well-behaved," Nate commented. "Guess he's trained to be."

"Yep. He's good with other dogs. Has a little more trouble with squirrels and rabbits." Jason looked around, liking what he saw. "Nice little town you've got here."

"It's quiet. Good people."

Jason appreciated both. No sirens, no car horns honking, no one yelling or fighting. No need to keep a lookout for shady characters who might want to cause trouble. Between his own size and his dog's, not many people bothered him back home, but every now and then a group of drunks or a desperate addict took a chance and tried to jump him. Which they always regretted, but the stress of the possibility meant it was hard to enjoy an evening stroll.

"So she offered you the job," Nate said.

"Yeah." Jason sidestepped a little kid who was zigzagging across the sidewalk, gripping Titan's harness handle hard to stay balanced. "It's just circumstance, I think. The other teacher had to leave in a hurry."

Nate glanced over. "Ashley wouldn't offer you the job if she didn't think you were qualified. She's real dedicated to her work at the school."

"Uh-huh. I could see that." Jason thought about Ashley, how she'd talked about the school. "We knew each other a long time ago. She's definitely more serious than she used to be."

"Were you a couple?"

"No!" The pastor's question made Jason's face hot. But ministers were entitled to be intrusive, he guessed. "Hardly a couple. She was married to my half brother."

"Ah. Did they divorce or…?"

"He passed away. Car accident."

"Sorry to hear it." He paused. "Would that make it hard for you to work with Ashley?"

Jason wondered the same thing. "I don't know why she'd want me for the job, aside from being desperate," he said. "I just finished my degree, and I'm messed up from my combat years." He nodded down at his cane and Titan. "I'm not a pleasant guy to be around, most days. If I ever was."

"And yet she offered you the job."

"Yeah." For whatever reason. Definitely not for old times' sake. He looked to the mountains, trying to absorb their serene indifference to the smaller concerns of human beings.

Nate seemed to read Jason's reluctance to talk more about Ashley and the job. "If you want good Mexican food while you're here, Café Aztec is your place." He gestured at a stucco building at the end of the row of shops, its little brick courtyard empty on this chilly day, but windows visibly alight with laughing and talking people inside.

A ridiculous vision flashed into his mind: bringing Ashley here for dinner. Seeing her dressed casually, with her hair down; making her laugh.

Completely ridiculous. He wasn't going to take the job. She'd offered it out of desperation, or pity. It would be hard to deal with that on a daily basis.

But this place... He looked around as they emerged from the downtown into a residential section consisting of small- and medium-sized wood-frame houses. An older guy, smoking a cigar on his porch, waved to them. Two little girls, bundled in winter jackets, rode bicycles in the street. A Steller's jay cawed from a fence post.

It was peaceful here, and Jason needed peace.

But seeing Ashley every day would be the opposite of peace.

"Here we are." Nate led the way up a stone walkway to a log-cabin-style home. Before they climbed the steps, the door swung open.

"They're here!" A boy of eight or nine yelled over his shoulder and then opened the screen door. "Come on in. Whoa!" he added when he saw Titan. "That's a big dog!" He didn't seem afraid, but neither did he reach out to touch Titan.

"He's a service dog, like Lady." Nate put a hand on the child's shoulder. "Landon, this is Mr. Smith. He might come to teach at Bright Tomorrows. And this is Titan."

As Jason greeted the boy, Titan lifted his head, sniffing the air.

Seconds later, a shaggy, cream-colored dog that looked like a poodle mix came barreling down the stairs and skidded to a stop at Landon's side, uttering a single warning bark.

"She's saying this is her house, that's all." Landon knelt and put his arm around the dog. "This is Lady. She's Mama Emily's service dog. That's a cool cane."

Jason blinked and smiled, already liking this kid. "Thanks."

The liking continued through dinner and expanded to include Emily, who was the reading teacher at the school, and Dev, who was a handyman there. The two of them spoke positively about the school, but they weren't overbearing.

"They met at the school and fell in *loooovvvve*," Landon said. "And I helped, 'cause Mama Emily had to tutor me."

"Nice." Jason scraped the last bite of beef stew off his plate and pushed his chair back a little. "That was a great meal. Thanks for inviting me."

"We're glad to have company."

"Tell me about the school," Jason said, just to be polite. He was pretty sure he wasn't going to take the job, but he liked these people and felt like he ought to at least pretend he was giving the place a chance.

He would've given it more than a chance; he would have taken the job in a heartbeat if not for Ashley Green.

She'd told him to stay away from her, back when he'd tried to help her deal with what had looked like a major problem with Christopher. He'd misread the situation, badly, and had promised to back off and stay away.

He didn't know if the promise should hold after Christopher's death, but he was pretty sure it should. For his own sake, if not for hers. Ashley was a dedicated professional woman, and an attractive one at that, but she brought out every single one of his insecurities: about his intelligence, his education, his level of success. Even about his morality, because he shouldn't have felt attracted to his brother's wife.

And then there was that phone call he shouldn't have made, right before the accident...

All of it had taken its toll, and he hadn't come into his own until he'd gotten far away from his mother and stepfather. And Christopher. And Ashley.

"It's a great place to work," Emily said. "So many kind people. Everyone pulling together to help the kids."

"It's not perfect," Dev warned. "Budgets are tight. And there are a couple of difficult teachers—"

"Like Mr. Stan, the math teacher," Landon burst out.

"Respect, Landon," Emily said. She frowned at Dev.

He looked apologetically at his wife. "I misspoke. There are some colorful teachers up there, just like anywhere else."

Emily smiled at him. "Exactly," she said.

Titan, now out of harness at Landon's request, chose that moment to get to his feet and locate the water dish Emily had put out beforehand. He slurped noisily and then looked around, muzzle dripping, creating a good-sized puddle on the floor.

"Sorry. Do you have a rag?" Jason started to stand.

Emily waved a hand at him. "Don't worry about it. We're used to dogs being messy."

Titan walked over to Lady, who sat close to Landon's chair. She stood as the other dog approached, stiffening.

Titan sniffed the poodle mix and she returned the greeting. Tails began to wag, and then Titan flopped down, and Lady, more delicately, lay down next to him.

"Titan can be Lady's boyfriend," Landon declared, and everyone laughed.

Car headlights flashed outside and then there was the sound of a car door closing.

"You expecting someone else?" Dev asked Emily.

She looked from Dev, to Nate, to Jason, her expression apologetic. "I did a thing."

Dev raised his eyebrows. "You didn't invite Ashley."

Tension rushed along Jason's nerve endings.

"Well," Emily said, clearly defending herself, "she's all strict and proper at school, but she's so sweet in person. I thought it would be good for Jason to see the other side of her." She looked at him. "I was totally intimidated by her at first, but she's a great boss."

"Does she know I'll be here?" Jason asked.

Emily looked even more apologetic. "No."

The doorbell rang, Landon and the dogs ran to answer, and Jason sighed.

This was going to be interesting.

Chapter Three

Ashley followed Landon from the door to the dinner table, sniffing appreciatively. "I ate at home, but now I regret—" She broke off, her step faltering, her mouth going dry.

Why was Jason here?

Her notion of a relaxing, companionable evening evaporated.

Just seeing the big man seated at her friends' dinner table made her heart race. She'd thought she'd handled her emotions, stored them safely away. But here, in a different setting, they came rushing back. Memories of their shared past sent hot blood to her face.

"No, don't stand up," she said, too late, but Jason, Nate and Dev were already rising, Jason a little awkwardly.

Landon scrambled to his feet. "I forgot," he said. "You're spozed to stand up when a lady comes into the room. Well, not at school, but..." He frowned.

"Socially," Dev prompted.

"You're getting to have very good manners," Ashley said. "But everyone sit down, please. I'm an old friend."

Especially in Jason's case. Although *friend* didn't exactly describe it.

"She's coming into the kitchen to help me fix the pie," Emily said.

"That's right." Because Jason was taking up all the air in the room and Ashley could barely breathe.

She followed Emily to the kitchen and leaned against the counter, crossing her arms in front of her. "You didn't tell me *he* would be here."

"Last-minute thing." Emily pulled a coconut cream pie out of the fridge. "Although… I admit, I did know the new teacher would be coming here when I invited you." She studied Ashley curiously. "I didn't know it would freak you both out, though."

"He's freaked out?"

"He was when he heard you were coming," Emily said. "Hand me those small plates, would you? Cupboard to the left."

Ashley was glad to have something to do. It gave her a minute to think.

Probably, this encounter was a good thing. It would let her and Jason get used to each other in a different context. See if they could handle working together or not.

She'd offered him the job, and if he took it, she would *have* to learn how to deal with him.

If only he hadn't come upon her and Christopher that long-ago day. Their argument hadn't gotten physical, but it had been about to. Jason, who always seemed to pay close attention to nuances—and to her—had seen something in her face.

It had been next to impossible to convince him that she was fine, that their marriage was fine. She still wasn't sure he'd believed her. After all, she'd never been a very good liar.

She'd moved on from those days of weakness, but seeing Jason brought it all back.

How much did he know about how things had deteriorated? How much did he guess?

Had he figured out what had happened in the final, fatal car accident, or would he?

Her stomach churned as she found forks and napkins and helped carry pie into the dining room. She wasn't going to be able to eat a bite.

Just get through this evening. It was what she'd told herself after the accident, in the hospital, facing the reporters, and her in-laws' blame, and her own grief. One day at a time.

She'd leave as soon as was polite and try to figure out what to do.

It was just that his presence had taken her by surprise. That was why she felt so disoriented. At school, she had more distance from her emotions.

After everyone ate pie, along with general conversation about the school and the area, they moved into Emily and Dev's comfortable living room. On the way, Jason gestured her away from the others. "Hey," he said, "I can see that I make you uncomfortable. I'm tied to Nate's schedule, since I'm staying with him. But I'll take off as soon as I can talk him into leaving."

His closeness made her swallow hard. "No, no, don't do that." She paused, breathed, thought. "I did mean it about offering you the job. I can be professional."

"When you're desperate to fill a vacancy," he said. He was looking at her closely, just like he always had.

He seemed to see what was in her heart, what she couldn't say.

And she couldn't pretend he was wrong. "I *am* desperate," she said, "and I'm also a little uncomfortable around you, but I trust that you'd do a good job." She did, too. She'd seen him interact with Landon, as well as Ricky earlier in the day. Despite his somewhat scary looks, he clearly got along just fine with kids. His recommendations were stellar and, with his background, he'd help to get that military program off the ground. "The school needs you," she said. "We need you."

"And you'd be okay working with me?"

"I… Yes. I would." She didn't have a choice, but more than that, she needed to be strong and put the past in the past. Working with Jason might help her do that. "Definitely."

He studied her for a minute, nodded as if he believed her, and turned and made his way into the living room with the others. Ashley followed, her heart pounding fast.

"If you accept the job," Dev said to Jason, "do you think you'd live up there?"

"Maybe there's a place in town." He was seriously thinking about taking the job, Ashley could tell. And she was equal parts glad and miserable at the notion.

"Not many rentals around here," Dev said.

"With the new hires, is there room in the staff cabins?" Emily asked. That was where she and Dev had lived before they'd married.

Living arrangements were the other problem with the whole situation. "Not really," Ashley said slowly. "The cabins are all full." She sucked in a breath, let it out and met Jason's eyes. "There is one option," she said slowly. "Matt and Missy are vacating their half of the duplex."

"The place we saw earlier?" He nodded. "Looked fine to me."

He didn't know she lived in the other half. And although Emily raised her eyebrows and nodded at Jason—telegraphing *tell him* loud and clear—Ashley couldn't summon up the energy or the courage to do it.

The next day, Jason walked into the cafeteria at Bright Tomorrows, Titan beside him. Surprisingly, he was feeling pretty good.

He'd wrestled with himself, talked to Nate, spent time on his knees, and it all pointed to one thing: he needed to take the job.

It was his best option for helping the kinds of kids he wanted to help and making a difference. Best for his health, too; being up here in the mountain air, away from city stresses, had already released the perpetual tension that had taken up residence between his shoulder blades.

The only thing standing in his way was his baggage: about Ashley, and his brother, and his own feelings of inadequacy and guilt. All of that could be dealt with. *Had* to be dealt with.

Jason had to be strong and courageous, as the scripture mandated, here in civilian life just as he'd tried to be overseas.

So, early this morning, he'd emailed Ashley to let her know he was accepting her offer.

She'd emailed him back, all very professional. She'd asked him to come in this morning to start his paperwork, which he'd done. Now there was a lunch meeting in the cafeteria to get the lay of the land and discuss the academic side, what he'd need to know about his schedule and his students.

He was reeling from the speed of it all, but glad. He wasn't a sit-around-and-wait type of guy, though he'd had to do plenty of it in the army. He was eager to get started.

The kids looked at him with open curiosity as he got a tray of food and made his way to the wall of windows at the back of the cafeteria, where Ashley had said she'd meet him. He was used to the stares. Today, he wasn't using his cane, but the combination of his own size, Titan's presence and maybe the tattoos that were visible in his short-sleeved T-shirt made him stand out. He nodded at the kids who caught his eye, and greeted Landon and Ricky, the kid with the broken leg, by name. He knew from working with juvenile offenders that earning kids' trust was a process.

He saw Ashley and his heart gave a little stutter. Today she wore a dress, prim and conservative but in a pale blue that he already knew would bring out the blue in her eyes. Her hair was clipped back on one side, soft-looking and shiny. An electric feeling zapped through him, head to toe. He wanted to touch that hair.

That desire would fade when he saw her every day. Wouldn't it?

And then he saw who was beside her and frowned. What was Captain Wilkins doing, sitting at the table with Ashley?

The Captain stood and shook his hand. "Hey, hey, looking good. This one finally saw reason," he added, clapping Ashley on the shoulder.

Ashley's half smile was not sincere. "Captain Wilkins

is the chairman of the board at Bright Tomorrows. Not sure if you knew that."

Jason nodded slowly. He'd hoped to avoid this kind of favoritism by arranging his own interview, but obviously it hadn't worked.

Her boss had made her hire him.

His enthusiasm about the opportunity took a little hit, but he remembered his decision process last night. It had been solid. He would go through with it, and make a success of the job, and the time to show that was now.

He set his tray down on the table, across from both of them. They made a little small talk while they ate their chicken sandwiches—one for Ashley, one for the Captain and two for Jason. To his surprise, the food was good, and he said so.

Ashley smiled, her first real smile of the day. "We're blessed to have Hayley McCoy in charge of the cafeteria," she said. "She knows how to strike the perfect balance between good nutrition and good taste."

"Including the best chocolate-chip cookies you've ever eaten," the Captain said, patting his less-than-flat stomach with regret.

Jason had scored two of those, and now he took a bite and nodded. "I'd take the job on the basis of these alone," he joked.

A couple of the boys came over to see Titan, and although Jason couldn't let them pet the dog, he explained that he'd be working here and would take the dog off duty sometimes to let them get to know him. Last night, Emily—his dinner host with the poodle-mix service dog—had explained that was what she did with Lady.

A bell rang and the cafeteria emptied, and the woman

Ashley had named, Hayley, came out to introduce herself and take their trays, waving away their offers of help.

"Ashley said she hadn't discussed the Young Soldiers program with you yet," the Captain said. "Let me tell you what I'm looking for. It's to encourage our graduates to join the service, up our placement rates, but it has to start way sooner than senior year." He showed them the website of a similar nationally known program related to the marines.

Jason studied the images. "You want the kids to drill?" He was willing but wasn't sure that was the right approach.

"Some of that, sure. Boys thrive on it," Wilkins said.

"But more about service projects and discipline and values," Ashley added.

"Okay." Jason didn't want to overpromise. "I'll look into it and put together a plan once I've gotten my classes under control."

The Captain shook his head, looking impatient. "We need to get this going ASAP. At least with an awareness of opportunities, meeting some veterans, that sort of thing."

Ashley snapped her fingers. "Veterans Day is coming up. We always do a little program, but maybe that could be expanded."

Jason was surprised she was taking such an interest. He'd figured she was just there because she'd hired him and was going to be his boss.

"See," the Captain said, looking satisfied, "that's why I want the two of you to work closely together on this."

Jason looked at the other man, confused. "But...she doesn't have..." He turned to Ashley. "You don't have any military background, do you?"

She shook her head. "None."

"But she knows the students here. You need an insider."

Jason looked off to the side, thinking. He didn't like how this was shaping up. He'd told himself he could do his job and keep a professional distance from Ashley, but if her boss wanted them to do a big project together... "I'm sure Ashley is busy with her regular job."

"Not convinced it would work," Ashley said at the same time.

The Captain looked at them, suddenly alert. "What's your history together?"

Jason was surprised the man had discerned they *had* a history, but he supposed it was bound to come out sooner or later. "She was married to my brother. Half brother," Jason explained.

"He passed away seven years ago," Ashley added.

Genuine compassion crossed Wilkins's face, making Jason remember he'd lost a son. "What was he like?" the Captain asked, looking from Jason to Ashley.

The question seemed to puzzle her. "He was...brilliant," she said slowly. "A concert pianist."

"Interesting." The Captain glanced at Jason.

"He got the brains and the talent in the family," Jason said.

"No. Uh-uh," the Captain said. "There are all kinds of smarts." He frowned. "So you two have known each other as in-laws for how long?"

They looked at each other. "We've known each other about ten years," she said. "I married Christopher nine years ago, but...we didn't have much time together before he passed away."

"Ashley and I didn't have much contact throughout

that time. I didn't get a lot of leave." Jason wanted to show the man that he didn't have feelings or contact or a connection.

The Captain didn't seem to buy that. Just like Christopher hadn't. Even though Jason had tried to keep his distance when he was home on leave, his brother had been the jealous sort and had sensed something, or thought he did.

Wilkins frowned. "I need to ensure that I have your cooperation," he said. "That goes for both of you. That you'll set aside any history you have and work together on this."

Jason looked at Ashley and saw the dread in her face. She didn't want to work with him.

She was the one who'd told him to stay away from her, but that had been about preserving her marriage. Things were different now.

"I can work with Ashley," he said. And it was true; he could. He could work with her despite the slight—sometimes strong—magnetic pull he felt toward her, a pull he didn't entirely understand.

If he threw his energy into his work, he'd forget about those feelings. They'd dissipate like mountain fog burned off by the sun.

He hoped.

Ashley looked down at the table and didn't speak. No assurances from her. The silence got loud.

The Captain slapped the table, loud in the now-quiet cafeteria, causing Titan to stand, alert. "This is the most important part of the job, to be blunt," the Captain said. "*Both* your jobs. This is what will help our placement rate and keep the school operational. I need for you both to be on board."

Ashley looked at the table for another few seconds and then looked at the Captain. "I can do it for the school," she said.

She wouldn't even look at him. She obviously didn't want to work with him. She'd only do it for the greater good of the school.

Why did she feel so strongly against him? What had Christopher told her?

"Good." The Captain stood and rubbed his hands together. "Now, I'm sure you, Jason, have to get back down to Denver and pack your things. Has she shown you your quarters?"

"Not yet," Jason said.

"Well, do that," he ordered. "Good to meet with you both." He shook their hands with his customary vigor and strode out of the room with a military bearing Jason could now only envy.

With the Captain gone, it got quiet in the cafeteria. A few clanks and soft acoustic music from the kitchen. Titan's sigh as he flopped back down.

"I don't necessarily need to see the living quarters," Jason said. "It's that place where the other teacher lived, right?"

She nodded. "Uh-huh. Bedroom and bath upstairs, kitchen and living room downstairs." She frowned. "Stairs aren't a problem for you, are they?"

"No. I'm more concerned about Titan. He's usually quiet, but if he thinks there's a threat, he's got quite a bark." He looked down at Titan. "Up," he said, and the dog lumbered to his feet. "Speak," he said.

Titan gave a couple of loud, deep barks.

A couple of the kitchen workers came to the door of the kitchen to stare.

Ashley waved at them. "We're fine," she said. She stood.

Jason stood, too. "Do you think he'll be too loud for the people who live next door? It's a duplex, right?"

She glanced at him and then down at Titan. "Yeah. It's a duplex."

"Do you think having a dog next door will bother them?"

"No." She was still looking at Titan.

She was acting weird. "Who lives next door?" he asked.

She drew in a breath and let it out in a sigh, and looked up at him. "Me," she said faintly. "I live in the other half of the duplex."

"You."

She nodded.

"So we're going to be colleagues, and working closely together on this Young Soldiers project. *And* living next door to each other."

She nodded and seemed to try for a smile, only it came out crooked. "Want to change your mind about the job?"

"Do you want me to?"

They were looking at each other and their surroundings seemed to fade. It was as if they were back in the house she'd shared with Christopher, staring at each other while murky, troubled feelings swirled all around them.

Now there was another factor, something almost electrical, because Christopher no longer stood between them. Jason could acknowledge what might have always been there: his awareness that Ashley was, in addition to being complicated and troubled and smart, a beautiful woman. He could admit how appealing he found her soft blond hair and those big gray-blue eyes that looked, right now, very concerned.

"If you can't handle having me here," he said, "I can still back off." He looked toward the door of the cafeteria, where a couple of boys had come in and were sitting at a table with an adult who must be a teacher or tutor. He felt a pang of regret.

He liked this place. He wanted to be a part of it.

But he'd already made Ashley unhappy and uncomfortable enough. If this was going to be a torment to her, he'd back out.

She opened her mouth and then closed it again.

He lifted an eyebrow and she looked at him steadily, and there was that little spark again.

She took a breath. "No," she said slowly, "I can handle it. Just because we're next door to each other, that doesn't mean we need to spend time together outside of school. And I can be professional, working on the Young Soldiers program with you."

She was setting a boundary, dictating that they were to be cool and distant and professional with each other.

He could handle that. That was the best thing. A woman like Ashley wanted a man who was cultured and brilliant, like Christopher. Not a big, damaged Joe like him.

"Professional," he agreed. He started to shake her hand and then pulled his own back. Couldn't start keeping his distance soon enough. "I'll be back up this weekend to settle in."

Chapter Four

As Ashley pulled into the unpaved driveway beside the house late Sunday morning, the usual glow she felt from church started to fade.

She should have invited Jason to go along.

He probably wouldn't have come. He's not the church type.

She parked her car, opened the door and just sat for a moment. The sky was an impossibly brilliant Colorado blue, and the air crisp, smelling of fallen leaves and pine needles. Both sides of the double front porch held pumpkins and gourds, hay bales and fall mums; she and Missy had decorated together.

Now the other side of the duplex was quiet.

He's probably not even up yet.

No matter, her guilty conscience scolded. She could have invited him the day before and let him make his own decision. She'd greeted him at one point during his move-in, made an offer of help that was quickly turned down. Pastor Nate and Dev had shown up to help him move his things into the duplex, and they'd waved away the idea that she could at least carry some boxes. She'd heard the three of them faintly, through the wall, the deep masculine conversation and laughs going on well into the evening.

It was good, the way Nate and Dev were already befriending Jason, making him feel at home.

Unlike you.

She sighed. “You’re not going to let me get away with this, are You, Lord?”

She looked over at the take-out container she’d gotten from the after-church luncheon. A hearty meal like that would probably be welcome to Jason, because with all the settling in, she doubted he’d had time to go to the grocery.

She’d give him the take-out lunch. She’d be a good Christian neighbor, although a distant one. She’d tell him about the church service and the lunch afterward, encourage him to come next Sunday.

For that matter, she thought, feeling better, Pastor Nate should have invited Jason himself. He surely had, so it was on Jason that he hadn’t joined.

So did she really have to take him the food?

Yes, you do.

Before she could talk herself out of it, she walked up his side of the porch steps and knocked on his door.

Titan’s loud bark made her jump. She heard a sharp command.

When Jason opened the door, she sucked in a breath.

His hair was rumpled, his flannel shirt unbuttoned at the top, his face sporting a distinctive stubble. All of it enhanced his bad-boy image. A lot.

He scraped a hand over his face. “Hey, Ashley. Wasn’t expecting to see you.” He made a gesture at his ragged sweats. “I’m not dressed for company.”

"I'm, uh, not company. Here." She thrust the take-out container at him. "I brought you lunch from church. Figured you didn't have much food in the house yet."

He took the container, peeked inside. A smile broke out over his face. "Smells like home cooking. I was looking at that can of corned beef hash sitting in my cupboard and thinking it didn't look all that appetizing." He held open the door. "Come in a minute?"

"I, uh… No, I didn't intend to stay. I just…"

"Come see the place."

He walked backward and she *was* curious, so she came inside. Titan came up beside her, his head higher than her waist, and she couldn't help cringing.

Jason noticed. "Side," he ordered, and Titan trotted away from her to Jason's side. "Sorry," he said to her. "I forgot you were scared of dogs."

"Not *dogs*," she said. "Just…big dogs."

"You were bitten, right?"

She nodded. "As a little kid." She pushed back her hair and turned her face. "It's not a bad scar, but the experience gave me a healthy sense of caution around dogs."

"Makes sense. I'll keep Titan away from you." He beckoned her in and pulled out a chair at his kitchen table, stacked at one end with boxes. "Coffee?"

"I… Okay." Jason was being hospitable, when she was the one who'd lived here first and should have been offering him the coffee.

He poured her a cup. "I have some boxed milk somewhere, and sugar."

She waved a hand. "I drink it black."

"A woman after my own heart."

For some ridiculous reason, that made her blush.

He leaned back against the counter, sipping from his own cup. "How was church?"

Her face warmed again. "It was good. I should have invited you to go. I just didn't..." She trailed off. She'd been going to fib, to say she hadn't thought of it, but she had. And surely it was as bad to lie about one's sins as to commit them.

Before she could figure out an explanation to stumble through, he held up a hand. "Look, I know things are awkward between us. And we have to work together more than we expected when you initially offered the job. Don't feel like you have to show me around and help me make friends." He gave her a half smile that made a dimple come out in his cheek.

How had she never noticed he had a dimple?

"Okay, good, but...I *am* your neighbor. If you need to borrow something or whatever, you can ask me. I... Just because of what happened before, that once..." She paused as the memories started flooding back in. "I know you meant well and I probably should have listened to you."

"I wasn't exactly using polite language. And I respect you for trying to keep your marriage together."

He was opening the door for them to talk about it, and she opened her mouth to say more and then closed it again.

She'd been a fool all around. In marrying Christopher. In letting him treat her the way he had. And then, at the end, being unable to save either him—because everyone deserved life, even an abusive husband—or her unborn child.

The room seemed to be getting warmer. A drop of sweat trickled down her back, then another. She glanced up at him, then down at the table. "I really don't want to—"

"Ashley. It's okay."

When had he gotten so understanding and kind? When had his eyes gotten that warm expression that said he'd suffered, too, and didn't blame her for how she was handling her own issues and losses?

Their gazes connected for a little too long. Ashley felt her breathing quicken, saw his eyes narrow speculatively.

She stood up, coffee in hand. "I should go. Thanks for the coffee. I'll, uh…I'll bring the cup back later."

He followed her to the door. "Thanks for the food."

"Of course. I'd do it for any new colleague." She had to negate the impression she might have given with that long soulful exchange of glances.

She was out the door when she stopped, something nagging at her. Speaking of new colleagues…

She should invite him. She didn't want to, but she should.

"Listen. Every Sunday night, we have a picnic or bonfire up by the cabins," she said in a rush. "You and Titan are welcome to come. But don't feel obligated." Feeling breathless, she spun and went to her own front door and inside.

The awkwardness and uncomfortable emotions of that encounter should show her, beyond a doubt, that she needed to keep her distance from Jason Smith.

On Sunday evening, Jason waited until he heard Ashley leave, and then waited ten more minutes before heading for the cabins himself. She'd been clear enough: this wasn't a special invitation to do something with her.

What had she said when she'd brought over the food? *I'd do it for any new colleague.*

She'd set a boundary. She wasn't treating him in any special way because of their history. That was only to be expected. It was good, really.

"We're meeting people, not hanging out with…*her*," he said to Titan.

The dog looked up at him with a knowing expression in his brown eyes.

Jason figured that the more people he met, the more diluted the impact of Ashley's presence would be.

She'd thrown him for a loop this morning, coming over in that fitted blue dress that brought out the color of her eyes and made her blond hair shine against it. She'd looked more relaxed and less professional than the two days he'd seen her at the school last week, but still classy.

Of course. Christopher wouldn't have a wife that was anything but classy.

Jason had always thought her pretty, and now, with her confidence and the depth of soul in her eyes, she was downright beautiful.

That didn't mean anything. It was just that Jason hadn't had a date in a year, not since he'd gotten serious about his education and his faith. It only made sense that he'd be attracted to Ashley. He'd be attracted to any good-looking woman who lived nearby, probably.

It didn't mean anything except that he needed to get himself out there, stop being such a loner, socialize more. Maybe there'd be some other single women here at this gathering. Maybe he'd meet a nice, good-looking, service-oriented woman who wanted companionship.

With a wrecked old hulk like you?

Jason stifled the inner voice, remembering what a therapist at the VA had said. *Isn't it interesting what our minds can do—take what was said about us in childhood and update it to include our present circumstances.*

He was disabled, had developed a darker view of life from all he'd seen overseas. But he'd also gotten a college degree and become a Christian.

I'm a new creation, he told himself firmly, and walked into the group of laughing, talking teachers standing around a bonfire as the sun sank behind the mountains.

He started introducing himself right away, to show Ashley—whom he'd immediately spotted over by the grills—that he didn't need her to help him fit in. And it was true. People were friendly and Titan was an icebreaker.

Nonetheless, within minutes, Ashley hurried over. "I'm glad you came," she said in her professional voice. "Let me take you around so you can meet everyone."

That went fine. He met a counselor and a couple of social studies teachers and an English teacher. All except one of the social studies teachers was male, which made sense, given that it was a boys' school. They all seemed to like Ashley, but no one looked at her in any possessive way. No one flirted.

That shouldn't make him happy, but it did.

They reached a spot where Hayley, the cafeteria head whom he'd met last week, was speaking with a tall, white-haired man.

"Stan Davidson," he said before Ashley could introduce him. "You look familiar, and I'm trying to figure out why."

Uh-oh.

This had happened before. Jason was pretty sure he knew what was coming next.

Stan snapped his fingers. "There was a show years ago about prodigies, and one of them was a pianist," he said. "They talked to his family, and it was interesting because..." He studied Jason. "You're his brother, aren't you? The soldier?"

"I am." Jason hadn't exactly been pleased with how the show had turned out, because it had made a theme out of the differences between him and Christopher. Christopher so cultured and talented, and Jason, the beefy hulk who'd gone into the army instead of college.

His own role had been minor, a quick interview. He'd participated because, back then, he'd still been foolish enough to want to make his mother happy.

He glanced over at Ashley and was surprised to see two high spots of color in her cheeks. And Stan wasn't saying anything about *her* connection with the piano prodigy. Interesting. Maybe she hadn't told people here that she had been married to a minor celebrity.

Hayley cleared her throat, her expression concerned as she glanced at Jason, then at Ashley. She, at least, must know the connection. "So, Stan," she said, obviously changing the subject, "what's your biggest tip for Jason as he starts his career at Bright Tomorrows?"

The tactic worked. Stan launched into a whole list of suggestions. Most of them were good ones, so Jason paid attention. And then the group gathered around a couple of picnic tables and feasted on grilled burgers and hot dogs, some kind of harvest salad, and caramel apple pie.

The talk got general. Jason heard more details about the school and the boys that he wanted to take note of. He wasn't exactly nervous about starting classes tomorrow, but he was aware that he had a lot to learn if he wanted to do the best possible job of helping these kids.

Emily and Dev, the couple who'd hosted him for dinner, showed up with Emily's shaggy service dog, Lady. Titan gave a deep woof, got to his feet and took a step toward her, even though he was in harness. Lady sat beside Emily, but her tail wagged furiously.

Funny. Titan usually didn't pay other dogs this much attention.

"Should we let them play?" Emily asked him. He agreed, and the two dogs sniffed and chased and played, running safely across the car-free dirt road, finding a vole and chasing it together until Jason and Emily called them back.

Both dogs were panting. "This is great for him," Jason told Emily as he filled a couple of paper bowls of water for the two dogs. "I did run him some earlier today, but the more exercise he gets, the better."

"Same with her," she said. "She's a high-energy dog. Is Titan?"

Jason laughed. "Not exactly. He's perfectly content to lie around the house for hours, but mastiffs have a tendency to put on weight. That's hard on their joints. So I try to keep him active."

"Anytime you want him to have a playdate, Lady is available," Emily said.

"And if we put Landon into the mix, everyone will get tired out," Dev chimed in, "which is a good thing."

"I'm sure." Jason liked the couple and had the feeling they might become friends.

Fairly soon after everyone had finished eating, the cleanup started. "We do these get-togethers to cheer ourselves up about starting a new workweek," Emily explained, "but the truth is, we all have class tomorrow, so we don't tend to make it a late-night party."

"Makes sense." Jason helped with folding up chairs and carrying them to somebody's pickup, and then spent a few minutes dousing the fire with Dev.

When he looked around, he saw that the cleanup was almost over. Ashley was helping Stan the math teacher carry a big box of supplies to a cabin across the road.

When she returned, Jason approached her. "Do you have someone to walk you home? I'm about to head out, but I can wait until you're through."

She tilted her head to one side, laughing a little, like he'd said something strange. "I walk home alone all the time. It's less than ten minutes away, and we're in the middle of nowhere. It's safe."

Hayley overheard and turned to them. "*I* don't like you walking alone," she said. "If I didn't live in the completely opposite direction, I'd walk with you." She turned to Jason. "The cabins are close together," she explained, "but with Ashley's house a ways off, I'm glad she has someone to walk with her. Especially on such a dark night."

It *was* dark. No moon. The sky was patterned over with more stars than Jason had ever seen in Denver. It rivaled the desert where he'd served. Was even better, because here you could look at the stars without worrying about getting shot.

"I'm fine walking home," Ashley said, her voice stubborn.

"I'll finish up here. You walk with Jason," Hayley insisted. "Emily and Dev will stay till we have the last few things cleaned up."

"Fine." Ashley sighed and fell into step with Jason. "I don't mean to be ungracious. That was a kind offer, but I really am fine walking around by myself. Don't feel like you always have to look out for me."

"Sure," he said, making himself shrug. It was clear she was trying to avoid his company, and who could blame her? He made her uncomfortable, bringing up all those old memories. Plus, the fact that he was attracted to her probably showed. Not so good.

She shivered and snuggled deeper into her lightweight coat. The urge to put an arm around her was strong. She was so tiny and pretty.

Stop it, he told himself. *You just need to start dating again.* He'd had trouble figuring out how to date and remain a good Christian, but he needed to work on that. Lots of guys managed just fine.

Meanwhile, he couldn't prevent himself from feeling protective of Ashley. Nothing wrong with that, was there? He slipped off his big down jacket and put it around her shoulders.

"You don't need to do that. You'll freeze!"

"I'm a heat machine," he said. "I don't get cold."

She glanced over at him and her gaze swept him up and down. She looked amused. "I imagine you don't, at that. You're pretty muscular."

"Glad you didn't say *fat*," he said just because her once-over embarrassed him.

"You're not fat at all!"

He shook his head, laughing a little, wondering how the conversation had gotten onto his body type.

Maybe because it was so different from Christopher's slim build.

He looked up again at the stars. He needed to have all this in perspective, and the stars, and God, were the only way to make that happen.

He found himself curious about Ashley, wanting to know what made her tick these days, the way a zoologist would be curious when he reencountered a rare species. At least, that was what he told himself about why he was curious.

He shouldn't be. He needed to keep his distance.

But they did have all that history together, and he wondered a lot about how things had gone with her in the time he'd been mostly away, before Christopher had died.

Her breath made clouds in the cold air, and she walked faster. Uncomfortable with him, maybe? Probably so. She'd always been the type to get all busy when she was worried or upset. "I remember when you took over that entire Thanksgiving dinner from Mom," he blurted out, and then wished he hadn't.

She glanced up at him, and he expected she'd look upset, but instead she wore a rueful smile. "She wasn't the best cook, was she? I mean, I'm no Gordon Ramsay, but I knew that turkey was going to be dry and Christopher would be—" She broke off and looked to the side.

Jason knew what she meant: Christopher would be upset. Maybe furious. Definitely out of proportion to the problem of overcooked turkey.

And from that one episode Jason had seen, he wondered how often Christopher had taken out his upset on Ashley.

But it wasn't the time or the place. They were almost to the house. "I remember the turkey…innards—whatever they're called—were still inside when you took it out."

"Oh my gosh, that was awful. Your mom took it hard."

She'd taken a lot of things hard. That particular day, she'd run upstairs crying.

Christopher had gotten mad, as had Trent, Christopher's father and Jason's stepfather, but fortunately, there hadn't been any blowups; they'd pouted and gone to watch a football game, muttering about calling out for pizza.

That had left him and Ashley in the kitchen, searching the internet for what to do about the situation. They'd neither one of them liked the idea of throwing away food. "When we pulled out that package of giblets and saw that it was wrapped in paper, it was like Christmas day," he said, grinning. "A little run to the store for some jarred gravy and we were almost as good as Jones' Market Thanksgiving dinners."

"Which isn't saying much, but it could have been a lot worse. We pulled that one out of the fire." They grinned at each other. Just as they had back then.

And just like then, something shifted between them. Jason snapped from the past to the present, where things were on a different plane. It felt like the mountain air got thinner. It was harder to breathe.

At the same moment, they both turned toward the house and walked up the porch steps. At her front door, she shrugged out of his coat and handed it to him. "Thanks," she said.

There was starlight on her face and awareness in

her eyes as she looked at him. The kind of awareness a woman had for a man. Wasn't there?

Or was he imagining it? She'd been in love with Christopher.

Their gazes tangled for a minute too long.

And then, at the same moment, they both came back to reality. The reality that they had nothing in common but history. The reality that she would never be interested in someone like him. The reality that, even if she was, he'd done something pretty unforgivable on the day her husband had died.

He cleared his throat. "Well. Better get some rest." He clicked his tongue at Titan, who'd flopped down on the porch floor as if they were staying.

Jason waited to make sure Ashley got safely inside and then headed in himself, trying not to think about what just had—and hadn't—happened.

Chapter Five

Ashley was doing her usual after-lunch walk-around, checking on things at the school, when Hayley hurried up beside her.

"I'm on my way out," Hayley said, "but I had to talk to you about last night. What happened?"

For a minute, Ashley thought Hayley meant that weird moment on the porch, when she and Jason had looked at each other in a way that made her breathless.

But, of course, Hayley hadn't been there for that.

"What do you mean?"

"What Stan said." Hayley shrugged into her coat. "Was your husband the piano prodigy in that show he was talking about?"

"Yeah." Ashley blew out a breath. "You don't miss anything, do you?"

"I could tell from your reaction. So that means… Jason was your brother-in-law?"

"Uh-huh." Ashley put out a hand to stop one of their younger students from running through the hall, checked to make sure that he had a pass to be out of class.

From open doors, classroom activity buzzed. Small

class sizes, students answering questions, teachers enthusiastic. Bright Tomorrows was a great place, good for the many boys who'd gotten off track and needed structure and extra support.

That was what she needed to focus on. Not the searching eyes and muscular physique of her former brother-in-law.

"How'd Jason end up here? Did you ask him to apply?"

"No way!" Ashley burst out and then, at Hayley's raised eyebrow, knew she had to explain. "I wasn't in touch with him. Didn't even know that's who was applying, because his application said 'J.C.,' but he always went by 'Jason' in the family."

"And his last name is so common." Hayley frowned. "So you didn't ask him to apply, didn't even know. Then how did he find us? Did he seek you out?"

Ashley shook her head. "He was as surprised as I was. Apparently, he'd come back to Denver after getting out of the service. He finished his degree there and wanted to work with at-risk boys. One of his advisers let him know about our opening."

"And there aren't too many places to do that, locally." They turned the corner, walking slowly now. "I'm glad he did. We needed him, with Matt leaving so suddenly."

One of the things Ashley loved about Bright Tomorrows was that "we." Everyone, from the secretary to the counselors to Hayley, the cafeteria director, took ownership. This place belonged to all of them. "I think he'll be good. Actually, I'm going to peek into his classroom and see how it's going." The industrial arts shop was in the farthest corner of the building.

"But things were rough with your husband, right?" Hayley persisted. She was one of the only people with whom Ashley had been open about her marriage. Not entirely open, but enough that Hayley had heard the general overview.

"Yeah. Nobody knows how rough. I kept most of it to myself, especially from the family. But Jason probably comes the closest." An image flashed into her mind. Christopher's fist, upraised. Her, cringing, waiting for the blow.

And a giant hand catching Christopher's, spinning him away, shoving him to the floor.

"So Jason knows."

Ashley nodded. She looked down at the scuffed floor. Someone really ought to polish it. She'd talk to Dev about it this afternoon. If he was too busy with other projects, she'd come over some evening and do it herself.

Yes, she'd do that. She wouldn't even talk to Jason. The project would keep her busy, and busy was good.

Hayley put an arm around her. "You know," she said, "you're not responsible for the fact that your husband hurt you."

Trust Hayley to bring her back to that difficult topic she didn't want to think about. "I know." She'd seen a counselor, talked it through. She knew, on an intellectual level, that it was common for women to blame themselves for abuse that wasn't their fault. Mostly, she didn't do that, not anymore.

But she couldn't forgive herself for staying with Christopher after she'd learned she was pregnant.

Her entire professional life was to make reparations for that. To make Bright Tomorrows a place where boys learned kindness and gentleness, so that they didn't turn out like Christopher.

So she needed to process what had happened last night and put it behind her, make sure everything stayed on a purely professional level with Jason.

"Is it going to be awkward for you?" Hayley persisted.

"No. We can't let it be. I'm glad Jason's here," Ashley said firmly. "Not just because of him filling Matt's place, but because he's going to help us beef up our military placement program. But..." She trailed off, unable to fake it with her good friend.

"But what?"

"But he brings up every awful memory I have about my marriage."

Hayley patted her shoulder. "That has to be rough," she said. "But there is one upside to the situation." She looked at Ashley, her expression quizzical, her lips twitching just a little. Hayley was the type who loved a joke.

"Go on—say it."

"On the plus side, he *is* superhot."

Ashley snorted out a laugh, because she hadn't expected that and because it was true, and then quirked an eyebrow at Hayley. "Are you seriously interested?"

"No, no, not for me." Hayley waved a hand back and forth. "I don't go for the bodybuilder type."

There was the sound of laughter, loud talking, some shouting. A dog's deep bark. General chaos, and it was coming from the shop classroom down the hall.

Across from the shop room, a teacher closed her classroom door with a bang.

"That doesn't sound good." Hayley checked the time on her phone and then looked at Ashley. "Do you need me to stay for backup?"

"No. Go. I'll handle this."

Or she'd try to. She hurried along the hall, waving an "it's okay" to Stan, who'd come to the door of his classroom and was looking down toward the noise.

She walked into the shop classroom to discover Ricky and another boy playing with Titan, whose service vest was rumpled and half off. Two more tween boys were tossing a wood block back and forth. Three others, a little younger, were at the computer, laughing at what must be some very funny videos.

Where was Jason?

And then she saw him, kneeling beside Langston Murray, a pale ten-year-old who'd just arrived at the school a week ago. The child was sobbing as if his heart would break.

Ashley flashed the classroom lights, causing a momentary break in the noise. "Everyone, to your assigned seats. Now."

The boys did as they were told. The only sound left in the room was the shrill, cartoonish voice of the video and Langston's sobs.

"Okay, boys, get out a sheet of paper and write down..." Ashley frowned, having few ideas of what they could write related to shop class.

"What you'd most like to build out of wood, if you could build anything you wanted to," Jason called. "And sketch it, too."

He spoke to Langston in a low voice, pulled out a folded bandanna and gave it to the child, and then guided the boy to the classroom door, where Ashley was standing.

She was already calling the school counselor on duty

today. "Ronnie? We have an upset student in the shop class. Would you be able to come down?"

"On my way," Ronnie said.

Ashley gave the boys in the classroom one final "I mean business" glare and then walked out into the hall with Langston and Jason.

"What's this about?" she asked the pair of them.

Langston shrank back against the wall and cried harder.

"Do you want to tell Dr. Green?" Jason asked. His voice was gentle.

Langston shook his head and turned away, wiping his eyes. He muttered something unintelligible. Jason leaned closer, listened and nodded.

"He doesn't want me to tell you," he said as he straightened. He lifted his hands, palms up. "I'm not sure what to do."

She couldn't approve his overall classroom management, but she did like his thoughtful and kind attitude toward Langston, a child she was worried about. She also liked that he hadn't immediately spilled the beans to her, destroying the child's newly forming bond with him.

On top of that, she was impressed to hear a man say that he wasn't sure what to do. That, in her experience, was fairly rare. Most guys pretended they knew it all, especially to a female boss.

"Ronnie, one of our counselors, is on the way down." She moved a step closer to the boy whose sobs were starting to subside. "Langston, Mr. Ronnie has a quiet, comfortable place where you can get yourself settled. Do you like dogs?"

In her peripheral vision, she saw Jason move to where

he could see the boys in his classroom and vice versa. No noise came from the room now.

"I don't like dogs!" Langston slid down the wall into a squat and wrapped his arms around his knees. "Especially that one," he added, pointing to the classroom.

Ah. "Yeah, I know what you mean." Ashley sat beside the boy on the floor, thankful she'd worn slacks today. "To be honest, I'm not into big dogs like Titan, either. They scare me. But Mr. Ronnie has a little poodle up in the counseling center who's very nice."

Langston shook his head. "I don't want to see it."

"That's fine. Mr. Ronnie's dog stays in her crate or her bed unless someone wants a cuddle."

"Are you talking about Snowflake?" Ronnie was there, kneeling on the floor beside Ashley and Langston. "Don't even think about seeing her today. She's been very, very naughty."

Langston looked up, seeming to be slightly interested.

"Why don't you come on up with me?" he said, gesturing to Langston. "You can take a look at her, but she is in her crate for the foreseeable future." He whispered conspiratorially, "The good news is, the other counselor, Ms. Harmon, brought in some sugar cookies, and they're fabulous." He kissed his fingertips.

"Go ahead, Langston," Ashley said briskly, standing. "You're excused from shop class for today, and Mr. Ronnie will decide when it's time for you to get back to your regular class schedule."

"Okay." The pair trudged off. Ronnie didn't put an arm around Langston. None of them had touched the child, even though he probably needed a hug more than anything else. It was a mostly firm rule, though, because a small proportion of their boys had experienced inappropriate touch or harsh physical punishment from adults in their past.

She wondered if Jason had managed to read through the entire staff handbook. Whether he had or not, he'd kept a good couple of feet between himself and Langston. He'd probably learned to keep his distance from working with kids in juvie, if not from the handbook.

As soon as Ronnie and Langston were out of sight, Jason spoke in a low voice. "I'm sorry I screwed that up. I'd like to get the boys back to their projects if there's time."

Just as he said it, the bell rang, signifying time for the next period.

Jason huffed out a breath. "Man. I'm not exactly winning the Teacher of the Year prize, am I?" He walked back into the classroom and whistled to get the boys' attention. "Okay, everyone. Put your names on the paper that you were working on and hand them to me on the way out."

Ashley stood to the side, watching, noticing how he greeted each boy, sometimes by name, other times glancing down at the sheet to get the name.

Once they'd all left the classroom, she smiled at Jason. "It's your first day. Relax. Do your best, and we'll talk after school about how everything went. Maybe do a little troubleshooting about what just happened."

"That would be great," he said as a couple of older boys came into the classroom, greeting Ashley and sneaking curious looks at the new teacher before slouching to their tables, some with phones in hand.

As she left the area, she felt a little bounce in her step. The reason wasn't hard to find. And it wasn't good.

Ashley needed to squelch the fact that she was slightly looking forward to the after-school meeting.

Jason walked toward Ashley's office at the end of the day feeling determined.

He was going to convince her that the bad episode she'd seen had been just that, an episode.

He winced when he thought about how she'd come in at his worst possible teaching moment today. He hadn't handled the classroom well, not at all.

There had been a few glitches the rest of the day, but overall, it had gone just fine. The kids were great, mostly full of energy, some a little mouthy, some sullen, but he felt like he could handle it. They weren't anywhere near as out of control as the juvenile offenders he'd worked with during his student teaching. And his leadership experience in the army had helped him know how to talk to the older boys, most of them nearing the age of the new recruits he'd sometimes worked with on base.

Teaching kids like these to work with their hands, to build things, was going to be satisfying to him and effective for them.

He just had to convince Ashley that he could do it, that he wasn't going to screw up on a regular basis.

And for that to happen, he had to forget about last night. Forget about that moment of looking into her eyes and thinking about how she was the type of woman he'd like to settle down with.

He might be able to convince her he'd be a good teacher, but there was no way he'd measure up as a boyfriend. He was way too rough around the edges compared to the man she'd actually chosen to marry. Christopher.

He was expecting an office visit, but when he reached

her office, she was talking to the secretary, Mrs. Henry, wearing faded, ripped jeans and a hoodie. When she saw him, she said something to the woman and then gestured him out the office door. "How would you feel about a meeting on the go today?" she asked. "I'd like to kind of supervise an after-school event that's being run by our new counselor. She's into horticultural therapy."

"Should I know what that is?"

She laughed. "I didn't. It's working with plants, and it's supposed to be great for mental health, which kind of makes sense. Are you good with meeting outside?" She glanced at Titan, then at Jason. "You're not using your cane today, but I want you to be clear with me if there are any limitations or ways we need to accommodate you so you can do your job. And that includes meetings like this."

He appreciated how direct she was. "I'm good today. Not for lifting Sheetrock or chopping down trees, but I can..." He trailed off, not sure of what they'd be doing. "Dig a hole? Rake some leaves?"

"Perfect. That's my level of expertise, too." She led the way to the back of one of the buildings, where six or seven boys were pulling dead plants from a flower bed and raking mulch. She spoke briefly to a woman who looked way too young to be in charge, and then led the way to a small, neglected bed off to the side. "I told her I have no green thumb myself," she explained with a wry smile and a shrug, "so she gave me an easy job."

She handed him a pair of gardening gloves, put on another pair herself and got down on her knees, tugging at dead plants and weeds.

He liked that about her, that she'd give her time to projects like this. He eased himself down beside her—

careful of his back, because when he thought about it, it was a little worse for the wear from standing in front of a class for seven hours—and started doing the same thing.

Beside him, Titan sat, alert, lifting his mighty nose to sniff the fresh air.

"I want to be here," Ashley explained, "because these boys are handpicked as being on the edge of getting expelled. Ms. Harmon maintains that she can get through to them through plants, so we're having a project. Clean up the old beds, build a greenhouse, start growing vegetables."

"Worth a try." He noticed a couple of older boys who had been in his junior-senior class. They'd looked bored and contemptuous then and they looked even more that way now. "Not a bad idea for me to get to know the boys a little, too."

And maybe that would help him to fulfill his goal, to be the consummate professional and show Ashley that he could do this job, and well.

"Those two," he said, nodding at the surly ones. "What are their names? Isn't the blond one called Flip or something?"

"Yes, and the other one's Ethan." She kept pulling out dead flowers, but looked over at him. "I noticed you were learning names quickly. That's great."

"Thanks. I want them to know I see them as individuals." And it was time to take the bull by the horns. "About what happened today. I didn't handle that situation with Langston well. I'll do better next time."

She nodded. "You were fine with Langston, seems to me. You connected with him and built a little bit of a bond, and that's important."

"Is he okay?"

She pulled out a big thistle and tossed it into the bin. "I think so. He spent an hour with Ronnie, actually got to know and like the therapy dog they keep up there. No more issues when he went back to class."

"That's good." He straightened, easing the pressure on his back. "I got so mad at the kids who were teasing him. I gave them a big lecture, but meanwhile, Langston broke down. Then I focused on him, and the others started acting up." He shook his head, annoyed with himself. "I need to multitask better."

"Not a strength for a lot of guys," she teased, then raised a hand. "Scratch that—it's sexist. What was your impression of Langston? He's new, and having a rough transition."

"I think he'll be okay." The kid's meltdown had to do with him missing his grandmother and his cats, and worrying about them, but Jason was promised to secrecy on those specifics.

"How would you manage your classroom when one boy needs attention next time?"

He thought about what she'd done. "I'd get them busy on something individual, something that didn't require much supervision, so I could work with the one kid."

"That's a good plan. Not a bad idea to have a few activities like that in mind for just that occasion. It happens a lot around here."

"I'll work on it." He got to his feet, grabbed a rake and started smoothing out the dirt where she'd pulled weeds.

"Your idea was a good one, having them say what they'd want to build."

He grinned. "Yeah, but you should have seen some of their answers. Not exactly realistic."

"I'm sure." She laughed easily. "Our kids have good imaginations. The realism will come."

She had a pretty smile. And he liked the way she thought about the boys. She was so positive, and it affected the atmosphere of the school.

She cleared her throat, her face going serious, and he realized that he'd been looking at her too hard. Staring. Doing exactly the opposite of what he should be doing, which was convincing her he was a professional who'd do a good job here.

"The other thing to do when you have a situation like that," she said, "is to call the counseling office. We have two counselors on staff, and one of them is usually available to come to the classroom and get a kid, help them out." She frowned, sitting back. "Everyone here, faculty and staff…we all care about the kids and try to help them however we can. But most of us aren't trained counselors. Sometimes the kids' problems go beyond what a layperson can deal with."

"I don't think Langston's were that way," he protested.

"Maybe not, but the other issue is that you can't leave a classroom full of students alone. Ever. Especially in shop, where there are all those tools and machines that could be dangerous."

"I didn't—"

"I know," she interrupted. "It's a compliment, Jason. You were exactly right not to let the rest of the kids out of your sight, even when you were occupied with Langston."

"Oh. Thanks." He felt sheepish, and again like he was losing sight of his goal. He wanted to impress her, and he realized it wasn't only because he wanted to keep the job, but because he wanted to impress her as a man. That was ridiculous and wrong. Compared to his brother, he wasn't impressive at all.

"So how'd the rest of the day go?" she asked. "How do you like it so far?"

"I like it a lot." He told her a little about the rest of the day, the various classes, his overall impressions of the boys. "I hope you won't hold that incident with Langston against me."

"It's your first day," she said. "Things happen. You're doing fine." She met his eyes and there was that slight little arc of connection again.

Thankfully, a noise from the group of boys broke the moment before it could get weird. The younger boys were laughing and watching the two older ones, who'd clearly done something wrong, because Ms. Harmon was lecturing them. She pointed to a pile of mulch and gave an order, and the two took the shovels and shuffled toward it.

"I'd better go see what's going on," Ashley said.

"Wait. I have an idea." He didn't know if it would work, but before she could ask questions, he stood and walked over to the two surly boys, carrying a shovel, Titan ambling at his side.

"Hey, Flip. Ethan. Want to talk to you about something."

They looked up.

He started shoveling mulch, wanting to set a good example of working hard. While he threw mulch into a nearby wheelbarrow, he talked. "You're both strong—I can see that. And the younger boys look up to you. How would you feel about participating in a Young Soldiers group we're starting?" Best not to call it a club; that was way too uncool for the likes of Flip and Ethan.

"What's it for?" Ethan didn't look at him, but he did take a small shovelful of mulch and toss it in the wheelbarrow. Progress.

"It's to encourage young men to consider military careers."

"How come?"

Jason reminded himself to be patient. "The military can give you a good start in life," he said. "That's how I got my start."

Flip looked from Jason to Titan, and Jason could almost hear the wheels turning. Jason *had* gotten a good start, but he'd also gotten a lifelong disability. That was a conversation for another time, so he hoped Flip wouldn't bring it up.

He didn't. Instead, he looked at Ethan and then back to Jason. "Will it get us out of this?" he asked, waving a hand at the mulch pile.

"Not today. But it might be an alternative at least some days. Are you interested?"

Flip shrugged.

"Why not?" Ethan said without a trace of enthusiasm.

"Good. We're in the planning stages, but I'll get you the information as we figure things out."

"Whatever." The boys turned from him and started shoveling, this time with a little more energy.

Jason walked away, unsure of whether that had been a good idea or not.

He hoped he hadn't just made his new boss even less happy with him.

Chapter Six

Friday after school, Ashley saw Jason walking out of the building, Titan beside him, talking and laughing with a couple of the older boys.

She hesitated only a moment before coming out of the office to flag him down. "Hey, Jason. Do you have a minute?"

"Sure." He spoke to the boys, waved and then walked toward her. "What's up?"

What was up was that he was one of the best-looking men she'd ever seen. What was up was that he was going to be great at this job; he'd done well this week, after that rough first day.

What was up was that she was having way too many feelings for a man she really ought to stay away from. And yet he was a man she *couldn't* stay away from, not after the phone call she'd just received.

"Listen..." she said. "I don't know what your plans are for the weekend, but is there a time we could meet for an hour or two?"

He shifted. Today, she noticed, he was using his cane.

"That depends. Am I in trouble?" He was joking, but she detected real concern underneath.

"Not at all," she reassured him. "It's just... I got a phone call from the Captain."

He looked blank.

"Thomas Wilkins," she clarified. "I was hoping to give you a couple of weeks to settle in with your classes before starting this military thing, but Captain Wilkins thinks Veterans Day would be a great time to kick things off and raise enthusiasm."

Jason frowned. "He's not wrong, but Veterans Day is..."

"Next Thursday," she said, nodding. "Less than a week away. Which is why I hoped you'd have time to at least talk about it over the weekend, set out a preliminary plan."

"I have time. Are you headed home? Could we walk and talk?"

"Sure! I'm sorry to keep you standing here. One sec." She went back into her office and grabbed her coat and bag.

She wanted to delay, to try to get control of the fluttery feeling in her stomach. It was so inappropriate. Jason was her employee and colleague, and she needed to be able to have a work-related conversation with him without melting like a marshmallow over a hot fire.

But she couldn't keep him standing there, especially after a long day at work that might have been physically difficult for him. She'd gathered that his disability included chronic back pain. She probably shouldn't have stopped him going home; she should have conducted this business on the phone, but it was too late to change her approach now.

So she locked up the office and headed out to where Jason stood waiting, Titan at his side.

They fell into step together, walking out of the building. The day had been warm for this time of year, in the fifties. Now the sun slanted low and the temperature was dropping.

There were a few people around. The boys Jason had been walking with had headed down to the residence cabins, and a couple of staff members stood talking beside their cars. A magpie scolded sharply from a wood-rail fence.

"I can meet anytime, to be honest," Jason said. "My plan for the weekend is to finish unpacking and settling in at the house, and get my classes ready for next week. So whatever works for you."

"No dates and parties?" she asked, only half joking. She'd wondered a little whether he would have friends up to visit from Denver. In the past, he'd been pretty sociable.

She'd also wondered whether there was a woman in the picture. Not that it was any of her business, but she'd expect a man like Jason to have a girlfriend. Had even wondered if he might have overnight guests.

Not your business, she reminded herself again.

"No visitors this weekend, and I'm not going anywhere." He hesitated. "Mom and Trent want to visit sometime soon, though."

That news hit Ashley like a blow to the chest. "Remind me to be somewhere else," she said. "I think I told you, your parents hate me." *Hate* was probably not the right word, but it was her shorthand to cover all the complicated, unhappy feelings between her and her former in-laws.

He opened his mouth to respond but she waved a hand. "For now, let's focus on the weekend and when we can meet." They were approaching the house now.

"I could make you dinner right now," he said casually, unexpectedly.

Ashley sucked in a breath. The offer was so simple, and yet not. "You don't need to do that."

They reached the porch and Jason sank down onto a step, wincing. He clicked his tongue to Titan and removed the dog's vest and harness, and Titan loped off to sniff around the yard.

He looked up at her then. "I didn't mean anything by the offer. I'm starving, that's all, and I'm throwing together some spaghetti. We could hammer out a schedule and see if we need to meet more over the weekend."

"Well..." Titan came over and sniffed her, and she held herself perfectly still. He seemed like a nice dog, but those big jaws could break someone's arm.

"He won't hurt you," Jason said. "And neither will I. I'm just offering dinner because eating on a regular schedule helps me with pain management. It's not anything more than that."

Her face heated. "Of course it's not. And that would be nice. I'm hungry, too. I can bring over stuff for a salad."

"Good. See you in half an hour?"

"Perfect." Ashley scuttled into her side of the duplex and pressed her hands to hot cheeks.

She felt embarrassed that he'd noticed her hesitation and correctly interpreted it as fearing he'd meant something romantic by inviting her to dinner—which, of course, he hadn't. Jason wouldn't want someone like her; she was weak. She'd stayed with an abuser, and as a result, she'd lost her baby. Of course, he didn't know that last part, but he had to sense her lack of strength.

Her shame about that ran deep, always under the surface, poking up to remind her that she was inadequate. Flawed. Just plain wrong.

That was how Christopher had seen her, too. She'd always fallen short of his expectations. He'd started homing in on that soon after they'd married. It was as if the intimacy of marriage had made him so uncomfortable that he'd had to push her away.

They might have been able to work through it, but Christopher's artistic temperament had precluded counseling. Delving into his issues would destroy his creativity, he'd said.

Without any help, though, they'd spiraled into a bad pattern of arguing, him getting madder, her getting scared. It had escalated into emotional bullying and, finally, he'd started to hit her.

By the time it had come to that, she'd felt like she was worthless, a horrible wife, not deserving of love or good treatment. The only goal she'd had was to preserve her marriage, and it had kept her in a situation that wasn't healthy. A situation that had, eventually, led to the loss of both husband and unborn child.

Now she leaned against her kitchen counter and sucked in breaths, trying to calm down and forget all the ugliness.

Jason's mere presence brought back the memories, because they'd all spent time together on holidays and he'd seen too much.

The sound of pans rattling next door made her stand straighter and make a plan.

Since the accident seven years ago, she'd focused

on finishing her education and then working her way up to the position of principal at Bright Tomorrows. She loved her work, loved leading the school to where it could continue to make a difference in boys' lives.

That was her meaning. Her calling. Her goal.

Tonight, that meant she needed to meet with Jason but remain impersonal and stay away from the past.

Twenty minutes later she was in his kitchen putting together a salad while he sautéed vegetables for his "almost famous" pasta sauce.

They'd both changed into jeans and sweatshirts. He wore moccasins; she'd left her shoes at the door and was working in her fuzzy socks. The sky was darkening now, but the kitchen was cozy, warm from the heat of the stove.

He added in some ground sausage and, within minutes, the aroma rose, making Ashley's stomach growl.

"That smells fabulous," she said.

"It's the secret ingredient, a mix of hot and sweet sausage. Just wait."

"I believe you."

They talked easily about his week, the boys, the school. Ashley was surprised at just how easily. Not only did they share the same workplace, but they had similar senses of humor, seeing the lighter side of working with the students while maintaining a serious, positive attitude about their potential.

It was fun. A lot more fun than Ashley would've had on a solo Friday night at her place.

It wasn't that she had no friends. She'd sometimes get together with Hayley, or with Emily, or both. But these days, Emily was often occupied with Dev, and rightly so, now that they were newly married. Hayley was wonderful, her best friend, but it wasn't right to burden a single friend with all your feelings and needs. Ashley had joined a book club in town and was looking to get more active in the church so that she'd make more friends and have more to do.

This cooking a meal in a warm kitchen with a good-looking man—this was a lot different from serving on a church committee, no matter how rewarding that might turn out to be.

She had to acknowledge it was better. It was more what she wanted. She'd always wanted to be married and raise a family, and although the kids part of the family idea was looking less likely, was it so impossible to believe that she'd find a relationship and marry again?

She dumped chopped radishes in the salad bowl and started peeling cucumbers. It wasn't impossible—all things were possible with God's help—but for it to happen with this man was definitely out of the question.

He knew too much about her. His family hated her. And what none of them knew was that she'd been carrying their grandchild. That was why she'd gone into a deep depression after the accident rather than try to patch things up with them.

"You got quiet," Jason said as he came over to the sink to fill up a big pan with water. "You okay?"

"Yeah. Fine." She took a breath and let it out, trying to let all her emotions escape as well. "We should talk about the Young Soldiers program, I guess."

"I guess we should, if your boss wants to get it started."

"I'd like to have a framework for the overall goal before we start punching in activities like a Veterans Day program," she said. "I'm not a fan of that rush-rush mentality, and to tell you the truth, I have some doubts about steering our boys toward the military."

"Why's that?" He put the water on to boil and checked the sauce.

"Because so many have come from backgrounds where violence and weapons were a part of life, a bad part," she said. "I'm not sure how the transition would be into making them see things differently."

Jason looked over his shoulder at her. "That's who's always been in the military, Ashley," he said. "The poor kids who didn't have another option. The kids who needed to get away from something at home."

"I guess you're right." She finished chopping cucumbers and rinsed her hands. "What about you? I never figured out how you ended up in the military. You certainly weren't from a disadvantaged background, although..." She trailed off.

"You're right. It was the 'although.'" He got a cutting board and sharp knife and sliced open a loaf of bread. "You know Trent always saw me as the weaker link. He was right, too—I didn't do all that well in school."

Ashley carried the salad to the table. "You did well enough to get a college degree, half of it earned online while you were in a war zone," she said. "You finished up with a solid GPA and great recommendations, both from your professors and your commanding officer." She knew all that from his job application packet. "That doesn't exactly sound like a weak link to me."

"Right, right." He waved a hand. "In most families, that would be fine. But when you compared me to Christopher, I never held up. I was the big, untalented kid. The black sheep."

Ashley looked away, not wanting him to see the emotion in her eyes. "In some ways," she said carefully, "you're a stronger and...and better man than Christopher was."

He didn't answer, and when she stole a glance at him, his jaw was clenched. He looked over at her, opened his mouth as if to say something, shook his head.

Instead, he got out plates and silverware, and started setting the table, and the opportunity to discuss himself and Christopher and her was gone. Probably for the best.

Soon they had big, steaming plates of spaghetti in front of them. He prayed over the food, a short but sincere blessing, and they dug in, talking about the school again, the kids, Titan. The present. No more of the past.

As they ate and talked, a comparison of her and Jason ran in the back of Ashley's mind. He'd so easily invited her in for a meal. He'd had fresh ingredients available, and although it was nothing fancy, he'd put together a nice meal in a kitchen that felt homey despite how recently he'd moved in.

He'd figured out how to create a good, sociable life for himself, or at least that was the impression she got from this evening. She, on the other hand, almost never invited people over, and she tended to grab meals from the school rather than do a lot of shopping. Her kitchen table was overrun with paperwork from school.

She could learn something from this man, if she could forget the role he'd played in her past.

Finally, she sat back, pushing her plate away. "I can't eat another bite. That was definitely the best spaghetti I've ever had. How'd you learn to cook?"

He laughed, carrying their dishes to the sink. "Self-defense at home. Trent and Christopher sometimes begged me to cook." He glanced at her. "Sorry to bring up those days again. I did some cooking in the army as well. Lived with a girl for a while, and she was another bad cook, so I developed my skills."

He'd said that so casually. *Lived with a girl.*

He must have seen her reaction. "I wouldn't do that now. Live with someone without being married to them. But a couple of years ago, right after I got out of the army, I thought it was no big deal. We were dating, and poor, and spending lots of time together. Why waste money on two rents?"

She nodded. She wasn't sheltered from the real world, even though most of her friends were Christian and didn't believe in living together outside of marriage. "A lot of people feel that way."

"Not a good idea overall. I know that now. But I did become a pretty good cook."

After she'd brought the rest of the dishes to the sink, he waved a hand. "I'll get those later. Let's get to work, hammer this thing out."

She'd brought over her laptop, and now she opened it while he got out a pad of paper and a pen. Titan, apparently discerning that there was no more chance of food being spilled, flopped down between them.

Up until now, she hadn't touched Titan. Standing, he was too big. But when he looked up at her with his warm brown eyes, she melted just a little. Hesitantly, she reached out and ran a finger over the big dog's head. "He's soft."

"Pet him all you like, when he's out of harness. He's a big baby."

Titan proved his owner's words true by rolling over onto his back, displaying his tummy, just like any small dog would do. He twisted his head to the side and looked up at her, as if to say, "I'm waiting."

She smiled. "Sorry, Titan, I'm just not ready to be that close." It was true, but she could see the potential. The dog *was* endearing, although huge. "Maybe someday."

Jason laughed and gave him a quick chest rub. "That's enough of that, buddy. Go lie down." He pointed at the folded blankets making a bed in the corner of the kitchen, and Titan, after a last hopeful glance at both of them, plodded over and flopped down. "Sorry for the distraction," he said. "Back to work."

"Right." She opened a new file on her laptop. "So if our goal is to inspire the boys to consider military careers," she said, "how could we make a Veterans Day program fit in? The ones I remember from childhood were more solemn than inspiring, and ours at Bright Tomorrows have followed that tradition."

"I know what you mean. Everybody's father or uncle."

"Right, or their grandfathers. You respected them, appreciated them, but you didn't necessarily want to *be* them."

"Right." He thought. "We need to find some young, cool vets to talk to the students."

"I think the boys find *you* pretty cool." It was true; she'd seen the boys watching Jason. Even in this first week, he was earning their respect, making them want to be around him just on the strength of his personality. She paused. "*You* could tell them about your experiences. That would be a simple program, but I do think they'd appreciate it. And then the fact that you're going to be running the Young Soldiers program—"

"*We're* going to be running it," he corrected. "And… I don't know. I don't love talking a lot about my time over there."

"But you're the perfect example. You were thought not to have the potential for college, and you went into the service, and you did great."

His mouth twisted. "Ouch. But you do have a point."

She'd spoken too bluntly. "I don't mean you really *didn't* have potential for college. Just that others around you, especially your mom and stepdad, didn't think you had potential." She reached across the table and gripped his arm. "You did, Jason. They were wrong about you."

When she touched him, felt that massive muscular forearm under her hand, the sensation seemed to travel from her fingertips all the way to her toes.

His arms were so strong. What would it feel like to have them wrapped around her?

Her face heating, she pulled back her hand. What had they been talking about? Potential. Jason. The students here. "People are wrong about our students, too," she said, and was glad she only sounded a little breathless. "I guess the hope is…going into the service is a way for kids who've been underestimated to prove their abilities."

"You're right." He sounded a little funny, too. Tense. "But the fact remains I don't like talking up my time over there, or being the main focus of a program. I could invite someone, a few friends, see who's around."

"We have no budget," she said. "We can't pay."

"Bricks without straw, huh?" He smiled.

The reference surprised her. "You know the Bible?"

His smile dimmed. "I'm a Christian and I can read."

"I didn't mean—"

"Sorry, sorry." He waved a hand. "I'm touchy. I was always the dumb one in the family."

She thought about Christopher, his flashy brilliance,

and compared that with Jason's quiet, solid manner. "There's smart and smart." She leaned forward, not daring to touch him again. "You're smart, and kind, and you're doing good work, as far as I can see."

Their eyes met. His were gray, flecked with gold. Striking, unusual eyes, especially in his square, strong-jawed face. She opened her mouth to tell him she liked his eyes and then shut it again. Not appropriate.

The only sound was the low hum of the refrigerator and Titan's sleep-breathing. And maybe, just maybe, the sound of Ashley's heart.

Abruptly, Jason pushed back his chair and got to his feet. "I'll contact my friends, see if any are free for Thursday's assembly." He turned and spoke to Titan, and the big dog woke and lumbered to his feet. "We'll walk you out," he said without looking at Ashley.

Okay, then, she'd been dismissed. She felt a little dazed as she stood and gathered her things. What had that been, that moment at the table? Was he angry with her or did he feel something else, something even scarier? She took a couple of deep breaths. "You're sure you don't need help with the dishes?"

"I'll get it." His voice was curt.

"Right." She grabbed her coat and laptop. "Let me know what you find out." She walked ahead of him, out of his place and into her own next door, feeling shaky and confused about her feelings as much as about his.

Monday after school, Jason was still disturbed by his Friday night with Ashley.

So much so that he'd simply texted her information it would be more natural to share in person: that he'd lined up two young veterans to speak at Thursday's assembly. By checking out the window and listening carefully before going outside, by staying away from church and the Sunday-night gathering, he'd managed to avoid her entirely.

She must feel the same way, because she'd answered his text with an "okay good" and hadn't stopped by his classroom today. It was awkward, though, because they'd have to talk to pin down the details of the assembly.

And now he couldn't avoid seeing her because there was an all-school staff meeting. Maybe that public encounter would ease the way into a nice, professional, detached one-on-one meeting.

In his school observations and student teaching, he'd attended a few teachers' meetings, and he'd heard about a lot more. Typically, they featured out-of-touch administrators droning on, laying out new and impractical plans, or criticizing the faculty for things that might or might not be their fault. They were the butt of many a teacherly joke.

The meeting atmosphere was different at Bright Tomorrows. He could tell as soon as he walked into the cafeteria, where the gathering was to be held. People milled around, talking and laughing. Boxes of pizza stood open on one long table, next to a cooler of soft drinks.

Hayley beckoned him over to the table. "Come and get it," she said. "Ashley orders food so people aren't starving, rushing home to cook dinner. And the cafeteria workers don't have to prepare it."

"Nice." And typical of her to be thoughtful of all the workers, not just the faculty. Grateful that he wouldn't have to put dinner together after a long day, Jason took a couple of slices. He spoke to Stan, and to Debbie, who taught domestic science in the classroom next to his.

"Okay, everyone, settle down and behave," Ashley said from a little stage. She was using a microphone, and her tone was joking, but people quickly found seats.

Jason found a table near the back of the gathering, intending to sit alone so that Titan wouldn't be in anyone's way. But it didn't seem to work that way at Bright Tomorrows. Hayley and Cletus, a quiet, heavyset man who worked in the kitchen, came over and joined him. Ronnie, the counselor, rushed in as Ashley was calling them to order and pulled up a chair to their table, too.

Seeing Ashley at the front of the room was a whole different experience. She was at ease. Funny. In her element. As she went through some business, dates, and plans, she was enthusiastic rather than droning, explaining why things were being changed or added to the schedule instead of just issuing commands from on high. She took questions and answered them thoughtfully. She seemed to really care about what the teachers and staff thought, and she encouraged discussion between them. She made them feel like a team, united for a common purpose.

She was a dream boss, a dream administrator.

And he couldn't help but compare the woman she was at the front of the room with the cowed, quiet, careful wife she'd been to Christopher. When had she changed?

If she'd been this kind of person when married to Christopher, would that have made a difference?

The answer came to him instantly: Christopher couldn't have handled her like this.

Jason's half brother had been brilliant and talented. Along with that had come the need to be the center of attention, everyone's darling.

And, he reflected, part of that had been putting other people down. Christopher had done it with Jason throughout childhood. Jason had ignored it, largely, and had chosen other activities to pursue—football and wrestling—that Christopher wouldn't come near.

But he'd felt the put-down, and Christopher had been charismatic enough that his view of Jason had affected their mother and Christopher's father, Jason's stepfather. At least, that was how it had all seemed to Jason.

Now he wondered. Had Christopher done the same to his own wife—put her down, made her feel like she wasn't good enough?

All of a sudden, he heard his name. At the same moment, Ronnie nudged him. "You're on, friend."

Jason blinked and came back to the present moment. "I missed it. What did she say?"

"You're to tell everyone about the Veterans Day assembly."

Indeed, everyone in the room was looking at him. He was definitely on stage, and he wondered whether Ashley had purposely thrown him under the bus because he'd been curt in his texts.

He shot her a questioning look as he got to his feet with an assist from Titan. His face and neck felt warm, both because of needing help and because of the unexpected public speaking opportunity.

So, as he cleared his throat, he kept his hand on Titan's head, and the big dog seemed to convey his own calm steadiness into Jason.

He explained the simple program he'd discussed with his two fellow soldiers, men he trusted and with whom he'd served. "They're younger than I am and didn't make a career of the military like I did, or tried to do," he finished. “That’s a more normal path almost anyone can pursue. We’re hoping it’ll be a good kickoff to a Young Soldiers program the board is asking us to develop, to improve postsecondary placement.” He looked at Ashley.

“That’s right,” she confirmed in that confident-leader tone. “Jason has the military know-how, and I’m bringing the insiders’ perspective. We’re excited to see how it goes.”

He thought he was done, but the Spanish teacher raised a hand. “Are they going to glamorize military life?” she asked. “Are *you*, Jason?”

Stan glared at her. “Or, on the other hand, maybe they’ll all emphasize how it’s way too hard for our boys. And yes, I’m being sarcastic.”

“Neither one,” Jason said, keeping his hand on Titan’s head. “The guests I’ve invited are going to be realistic, as am I. We don’t want young men to enlist expecting something different from what they’ll actually get.”

Someone started humming a jingle from an old army recruitment commercial, and a few people laughed, lightening the atmosphere. “Hopefully, we’ll have more depth than a thirty-second advertisement,” Jason said. “And we’re also hoping the program will be beneficial to a good number of the boys, whether or not they end up enlisting. The assembly, too, so…” He looked up at Ashley. “Will everyone be required to be there, or should we ask that our colleagues steer students toward it?”

“It’s an all-school assembly. But teachers can help by talking it up.” She smiled at him, and it was like the sun breaking out from a cloud bank.

“One objection,” Stan said. “I understand you invited

Flip and Ethan to participate. Not to cast shade on our troubled students, but was that a good idea?"

"Boys like that need a chance," Jason said firmly. He felt no ambivalence about it.

"And attendance is optional, once the Young Soldiers program starts," Ashley chimed in. "If they're not motivated, they don't have to join."

"Attendance was by invitation, but optional at my horticulture therapy program, too," Ms. Harmon, the new counselor, said. "They chose to come and they chose to disrupt it. I had to remove them today."

Ashley's confident expression faltered, and a few staffers were talking among themselves.

"Look, the Young Soldiers program is an experiment," Jason said, a little loudly to regain people's attention. "There are bound to be some glitches. We're open to feedback from anyone, so be in touch." He paused, then added, "I'm in the shop room, teaching kids to play with dangerous machines."

Everyone laughed, and Jason was relieved to be able to break the tension. Still, the meeting had put a different spin on things.

This Veterans Day program, and the whole Young Soldiers program, was pretty much on him. Not only that, but there were dissenting voices at the academy, people who weren't on board with the plan.

He had to step up, work with Ashley no matter how difficult, because it was very possible that their new initiative could be a disaster.

Chapter Seven

Even though the assembly had been going well, Thursday afternoon, Ashley couldn't relax.

The boys were surprisingly quiet and attentive, listening to veterans not much older than some of them were. The men who'd come to participate in the event didn't sugarcoat the stress, the dangers, even the boredom, of working in a war zone, but they also made it clear they were glad they'd served.

It was going great, actually. She should be enjoying the success of this first Young Soldiers event.

But what she hadn't expected was for all three to show up in uniform. What she hadn't expected was how good Jason would look in uniform.

They'd all worn camouflage, not dress uniforms. Ordinary army boots. They'd explained that they wanted to show the boys the day-to-day, not the ceremonial side you saw on TV or at military funerals.

Still, they all looked impressive. Jason especially.

And it wasn't just looks. A subtle change had come over Jason, in a military role, in uniform, with his fellow soldiers. He had, it turned out, been their leader, had risen to the rank of corporal and had been working on his degree with the thought of rising further, before his injury.

He spoke of that without self-pity, but she realized for the first time what a significant loss he'd faced; how his promising military career trajectory had been cut short.

As the young soldiers told of Jason's heroics, asked him to show off his medals—which he did, reluctantly, quickly taking the spotlight off himself and putting it back onto the whole unit—she saw a different side of him. A quietly impressive side.

He asked for a moment of silence for those who'd given their lives, and it was so quiet you could hear the sound of Titan's breathing.

When they opened up the floor for questions, the boys were full of them.

"Were you scared?" was the first one.

"They weren't scared," another boy said.

The three soldiers looked at each other. "Were you scared?" one of the visitors asked the other.

"Totally," the other said. "I was terrified half the time over there."

"Me, too," said the one who had asked.

"Me as well," Jason said, which caused a murmur among the boys.

"Nelson Mandela said that, 'Courage was not the absence of fear, but the triumph over it,'" Stan called from the audience.

A couple of the faculty gave him irritated glances—Stan did tend to have advice and an opinion about everything—but in this case, Ashley felt he was entitled to share his view. Stan was a veteran as well, and his quote was a good one.

"Were there girls around?" one of the older boys asked, causing others to snicker. That was one of their main objections to attending Bright Tomorrows, that there were no girls.

Ashley opened her mouth to scold, but before she could start, the veterans at the front of the room responded better than she could have, telling of the valor of the female soldiers in their unit.

Finally, they had to cut off the questions. Ashley headed to the front to thank the men, asking for another round of applause for them and for all who'd served. Then she capitalized on the moment. "There's a sign-up sheet up here, or there will be in five minutes," she said, waving to Mrs. Henry, "if you want to join the first group of Young Soldiers. Anyone's eligible."

Mrs. Henry, who tended to think of everything, waved a legal pad, and students crowded near her, talking with more enthusiasm than Ashley had ever expected.

Ashley stepped to the side and thanked their guests. "Pretty sure you did an overly good job," she said, gesturing to the mob around Mrs. Henry. Then, to Jason, "This might be bigger than we anticipated."

There. She'd sounded cool and objective when speaking to this incredibly handsome and brave man.

"I can come up once a month and help," one of the men, Tyler, said.

"Not me. I've got two little ones at home and my wife would have my hide if I made this a regular escape."

"Speaking of escape," Tyler said, looking at Jason, "come out for a brew? I'm sure there's a bar even in this Podunk." Then he seemed to realize Ashley was still there. "Sorry, miss. You're welcome to come, too."

"Thanks, but I'll leave you to it," she said.

"Jason?"

"Can't combine my pain meds with alcohol," he said. "And the truth is, I've lost my taste for it."

She noticed that Flip and Ethan were listening. Good. They needed to hear that drinking and partying weren't necessary to be an adult. A man. A soldier.

As the crowd dissipated, Ashley and Jason fell into step together. "That was really good," she said. "You were impressive. I had no idea about your medals, though it doesn't surprise me you got them." It didn't surprise her because she knew how protective he was, how much he cared for others.

He shrugged. "I did my job. Hey, listen, Ashley, I have something to ask you."

Her heart gave a little jump, one she scolded it for. This was probably work-related.

"I, uh…I got a call from my stepfather last night. Apparently, Mom is having some problems. Health problems."

"I'm sorry to hear it." She was, although she didn't know quite why he was telling her this, since she and her former in-laws weren't on speaking terms.

"They want me to come down to Denver for Thanksgiving dinner."

"Of course. You're off that whole week."

He laughed ruefully. "Part of a day is all I can manage with them." Then his face went serious. "When I told them I was working with you…they asked if you could come, too."

She stopped right there in the empty hallway and stared at him. "What? Why?"

"I'm not sure. My impression was that Mom feels

bad about some of the things she said when Christopher died. Or about shutting you out afterward."

Ashley drew in a breath and let it out slowly. There had been a time when she'd wished she could reconnect with them and grieve together, but that time was long past. "I don't know, Jason. There's so much history between us."

He held up a hand. "Don't decide now. I figured you'd be ambivalent at best. That's why I wanted to tell you early, so you could have a little time to think it over."

Someone called Jason's name and he turned with a wave and was gone.

Leaving Ashley to her spinning thoughts and doubtful worries. She shouldn't go to visit her former in-laws. Shouldn't reopen those old wounds.

Shouldn't let the fact that it would involve a day trip with Jason influence her decision either way.

Should she?

Ashley was still pondering that question almost a week later as she walked over to the school on Wednesday evening. Around her, thick, wet flakes of snow rained down. It dampened the road and coated the school's grassy lawn already, and it was predicted to snow all night.

She pulled the hood of her jacket tighter in an effort to stay warm and save her hair from getting soaked. Not that it mattered; it was just going to be her and Hayley decorating the cafeteria for Friday's all-school Thanksgiving luncheon.

After that, most of the boys would go home for a week with their families. Only a few couldn't go, due to family issues or logistics. Ashley had pretty much decided she would stay on campus to help with them.

That was her responsibility. Not meeting up with the in-laws who'd treated her badly and who were sure to scratch at old wounds.

She'd determined to talk to Hayley about it. Hayley knew more than anyone else about her marriage and its aftermath. If Hayley agreed that staying away from the family event was the right thing to do, Ashley would be able to eliminate the small nagging sense of guilt she felt.

After shaking the snow from her coat and stomping away what had accumulated on her boots, she walked through the doors that led directly from outside into the cafeteria.

"Hey, girl, get in here where it's warm. Sort of." Hayley was bundled in a thick sweater and jeans. They didn't heat the big cafeteria as much as the rest of the school. "I'm about ready to skip Thanksgiving and move right on to the Christmas decorations."

"No, we have to do Thanksgiving first. The boys expect it." She draped her coat over an empty chair. "Will you have time to decorate for Christmas, though? Aren't you headed to see family back East over the holiday?"

Hayley shook her head. "My invitation fell through. I'm staying. So there will be plenty of time for me to get a start on Christmas decorations."

"Oh, well, I can stay, too. I'll help you."

Hayley shook her head. "No, because you're staying through Christmas, right?" They all took turns so that the boys who couldn't go home had some staff on hand, both to supervise and to cheer them up and find things for them to do.

"I can stay both," Ashley said firmly. It was better than driving for hours to visit her aunt and uncle and cousins, like she sometimes did. She never felt like she fit in there, anyway.

Hayley tilted her head to one side, a cornucopia table decoration in her hand. "You sound funny. What's going on?"

Ashley pulled a stepladder over toward the entryway to the food service area. "I did get an invite," she said, trying to sound offhand. She found the box labeled "Thanksgiving Garland" and dragged it in the same direction.

"To do what?" Hayley was stretching orange plastic sheeting over a long table.

"To go with Jason to have a meal with my former in-laws."

"What?" Hayley straightened and stared. "I thought you and they didn't get along."

"We don't, and that's why I'm not going to go." Ashley tugged at the first strand of garland, laden with fake leaves and plastic pumpkins, and started untangling it.

Hayley trimmed the makeshift tablecloth and attached it with clips. "Wonder why they invited you?"

Good, Hayley wasn't urging her to accept the invitation. "I guess because my mother-in-law, Marsha, is ill, she feels bad about how she treated me. Or at any rate, she wants to see me. Maybe she has questions about Christopher, which I do *not* want to answer." She yanked hard on the garland, finally freeing it from the tangle, and started up the ladder.

"How *did* she treat you? And why?" Hayley moved on to the next table and started unrolling more orange plastic. "Not that it's any of my business."

Ashley attached garland to the top corner of the entryway. "Does that look good?"

Hayley came over and tugged it down a little. "There. And let me hold the ladder. We don't need our fearless leader to be injured, especially when the weather's too bad to run you to the ER."

"Good point." Ashley twisted the garland into place. "Hand me the next strand, will you? I'll get it started here."

Hayley tugged out another strand and held it up to where Ashley could grab it. "So you don't want to talk about your mother-in-law."

"I can talk about it." Especially when she wasn't looking directly at Hayley. "She blamed me for the accident. Basically, for killing..." Her throat went tight, but she pushed out the rest of the words. "For killing her son."

Hayley was quiet a minute. "*Was* it your fault?"

A flash of memory flickered through her head, more of an image, really. Her telling Christopher her news. Their loud, accusatory argument. Him reaching over and grabbing her hair, pulling it hard, yelling that it wasn't supposed to happen. She hadn't defended herself, not really. She'd been focused on the road, screaming at him to be careful, to brake, to pull over.

And then had come the crash that had destroyed their lives. "Who knows? I guess you could say it was both of our faults," she said, trying for a breezy tone that fell totally flat.

"Were you driving?"

"No. But I...I brought up a difficult topic, even though I knew how volatile he was." Her voice tightened. She draped the strand of garland over a nail she could barely see through a blur of tears.

"Come down," Hayley said, and when Ashley didn't immediately obey, she spoke again, more firmly. "Come on down now, Ash. This isn't safe."

Hayley was right. Ashley gave the garland a final tug, making sure it was secure, and then made her way down the ladder.

As soon as her feet hit the floor, Hayley grabbed her hand and pulled her to one of the orange-clad tables. "Do you want to talk about it more or should I shut up?"

Ashley shook her head, rapidly. "I can't. Not right now."

"That's fine, but have you talked to anyone?"

She shrugged. "A social worker." She remembered the harassed, overly busy woman who'd come in after she'd regained consciousness in the hospital to tell her what had happened. To explain that she'd lost both her husband and her unborn child. Despite the fact that she couldn't stay long, the woman had gotten tears in her eyes and held Ashley's hand while delivering the miserable news.

"And you still feel guilty," Hayley said. "And that's maybe why you work all the time and never have fun and can't move on." She handed Ashley a napkin.

Ashley blew her nose and wiped her eyes. "Is that true? Am I really that much of a drag?"

"It's true, but not in a bad way," Hayley said. "You have fun, and you *are* fun, but you're always holding something back." She leaned forward. "And you know what? I think going to see your former in-laws might be a way to fix it."

Ashley blinked. "Are you kidding? I'm pretty sure

going there to get beat up again will make things worse, not better."

"But maybe they won't beat you up. Maybe your mother-in-law wants to make amends, and it would be good for you both."

That was…possible. Not likely, but possible.

It would also be a way to spend more time with Jason. At the thought, longing filled her heart. He really was a wonderful, admirable man.

"And you could spend more time with Jason," Hayley said in an eerie echo of Ashley's thoughts.

The scenario played out in Ashley's mind. She could go with Jason, drive with him to Denver, spend Thanksgiving Day with him.

And Mr. and Mrs. Green.

Letting him find out more about the disaster that had been her marriage, the disaster of the car wreck and the losses that had followed.

"Is your mother-in-law a horrible person?" Hayley persisted.

"No. No, not horrible." She was just oblivious to her younger son's flaws.

"Uh-huh. And she's sick. How sick?"

"I don't know. Jason didn't know. I think it's serious."

Hayley stood and brought a cornucopia decoration to the table where they were sitting and started arranging it. "Well, for what it's worth, I think you should go."

"I can't!"

"It's the right thing to do," Hayley continued as if Ashley hadn't spoken. "For her, and for your father-in-law, but more importantly, for you. You need to move on from the past."

"I—" She broke off. "Maybe I'll think about it."

"You do that," Hayley said. She squeezed Ashley's shoulder on her way to the decoration boxes.

Ashley stood and went back to work, too.

A part of her knew Hayley was right. She needed to move on, get past the past.

But if moving on was moving *through* the memories, the sadness…that was harder.

That, she didn't know if she'd *ever* be ready to do.

Chapter Eight

This was a mistake.

Jason glanced over at Ashley, tense in the passenger seat. Then he returned his attention to the winding mountain road.

Up ahead, a snowcapped peak jutted against the sky. Ponderosa pines lined the road, interspersed with white-trunked aspens, and a hawk soared overhead.

Gorgeous, sure, which was why he'd taken the scenic route. He hadn't considered that it meant more time in the car with Ashley. Tension came off her in waves, thick enough that he could feel it himself. Or maybe that was his own tension knotting his stomach.

He was trying to be a good son, a good friend, a good Christian, by making this trip and bringing Ashley along. But it wasn't easy.

He wanted to ease Ashley's tension. He *needed* to focus on friendship with her, rather than how pretty she looked in her denim skirt and boots and a blue sweater that fit her like it had been tailored to her exact form.

"Good thing you have four-wheel drive," she said

as he turned on the windshield wipers. "Those clouds don't look good."

"It'll clear up when we get closer to Denver." Like any self-respecting guy planning a trip, he'd spent an hour watching the weather channel this morning.

"Are you sure? Maybe we should turn back."

"It won't be that bad."

She gave a humorless laugh. "Are you talking about the roads or the visit?"

"Both?" He steered around a curve. The peaks ahead blurred in heavy clouds. "At least, I hope so. I know for sure the drive isn't going to be a problem. The roads are just wet."

"They'll freeze on the way home," she fretted, and then turned to him. "What if we have to stay the night?"

Jason was pretty sure her worries had little to do with the weather and everything to do with seeing Mom and Trent for the first time since shortly after Christopher had died. He found himself wanting to comfort her. "Not happening. This is strictly a one-afternoon visit. We can use the roads as an excuse to leave ahead of time, if things get rough."

Ashley was quiet for a few seconds. "Okay. That's a good plan."

They drove quietly. Classical music—Ashley's choice—played on the radio. It would've been peaceful if he wasn't dreading the visit to come.

Of course, he was worried about his mom. Though their relationship hadn't been perfect, she'd brought him into this world and he loved her. The fact that she wanted to see Ashley as well as him—did it mean the illness his stepfather had downplayed was actually serious?

He couldn't believe it would be; Mom had always

been so healthy. More likely, she was getting older and recognizing that she wanted her family around her, and wanted to make amends for mistakes she'd made.

Jason would support her in doing that, but he didn't expect an enjoyable family holiday, that was for sure.

On the few occasions he'd visited his mother and stepdad in the years since Christopher's death, they'd avoided the subject of his brother. But pictures of him held positions of honor on the walls of the living room, up the stairs, and on the entryway table, alongside a few pictures of Jason, wearing either a football or a military uniform.

Jason knew he should be over feeling inadequate compared to Christopher, but the truth was, he wasn't there yet.

The clouds were thinning out now, and when the sun broke through, casting golden rays, more of the distant peaks came into view.

"Wow, so pretty," Ashley said softly.

When he glanced over, he liked the soft expression that had replaced the worried one on her face.

When he saw a scenic overlook sign, he pulled off. "Mind if we take in the view for a few minutes?"

"No! I don't mind. Anything to delay what's coming." She tucked a leg under her and sat straighter, looking out at the distant mountains.

Way in the distance was the Denver skyline. Jason rolled down his window, and crisp mountain air carried in the fragrance of snow and pine. "Too cold?" he asked.

"No. Let's get out and look." She was opening the door and climbing out before he could get around to her side of the vehicle to help her. Not that she needed help, but he tried to retain the manners of a gentleman as much as he could, given his slowed pace of movement.

He opened the rear door and let Titan out, holding onto his lead as the dog spotted a chipmunk and pulled toward it. "Whoa, buddy, no hunting today," he said firmly. Titan out of his service vest was a normal dog. He wanted to run and chase.

Ashley stood, small in her big puffy coat, looking out. "So pretty," she said. "Jason, why did your parents treat Christopher so much better than they treated you?"

He hadn't expected that question. "You noticed," he said wryly, trying to make a joke of it.

"Of course I noticed. I realize you weren't Trent's biological child, but was there more to it?"

He'd asked himself that question many times. "I think… Mom wanted to put the past behind her. I was the reminder of it. And Trent liked to pretend she'd never been with anyone but him, but there I was in his face."

"How old were you when they married? You must have been pretty young."

He leaned against a wooden sign that informed tourists about the view. "I was two, and a difficult kid."

She smiled. "Aren't all two-year-olds difficult?"

"Right." He shrugged as if he didn't care. "It doesn't make a whole lot of sense." Except it did make sense. Christopher had been small and easy to manage, a little sickly, so he'd required extra attention and pampering. Whereas Jason was strong as a horse and almost as big as one. "Mom's main fear was that I would bully Christopher because I was so much bigger than he was. But in reality—" He broke off. This was her late husband they were talking about.

"In reality, he was a bully," she said quietly.

"He became one, yeah. If you never hear the word

no and your parents idolize you, it's hard to become a good human being. Plus, the idolizing went on outside of the family, too, because he was so talented."

"Were you jealous?" she asked.

"As a young kid, sure I was. I wanted that kind of attention for myself." He laughed a little. "Of course, I didn't have a good way of asking for it. It was the classic 'bad attention is better than no attention' situation."

"You got in trouble."

"A lot, for a while." He turned the conversation back to her. "That one time when I came upon you two fighting..." It was a scenario he'd wondered about ever since; wondered if he should have forced an intervention. "Was he going to hurt you? You insisted then that he wasn't, but I had my doubts."

She looked away, out toward the distant peaks. "Yes."

"Did he hurt you other times?"

She didn't speak, but the hood of her coat moved in a tiny nod.

Hot rage flooded him. "I told you to tell me if anything happened. You said you would."

She cringed away from him, and he realized he'd raised his voice and that he was looming over her.

He lifted his hands and backed a few steps away. "I'm sorry. I would never hurt you. I give you my word about that. But it burns me up, what he did."

"I knew it would," she said softly. "I also knew that you were overseas fighting bad guys. I should have been able to handle it myself. Should have left and..." She blinked back tears. "You don't know how much I wish I'd left."

He wrapped his arms around her and pulled her

loosely against his chest, just for a second. The urge to comfort her was strong. But he didn't want to trap her, to touch her against her will, after what Christopher had done.

She sniffled and pulled back. "I'm not normally such a dishrag," she said, wiping her eyes on her gloves.

"You've recovered from what happened, you think?" he asked. He was reaching for conversation that would keep him from reflecting on how good it had felt to hold her.

She shrugged. "Not really. But you go on."

That seemed like a funny way to put it. "Did you still love him by the time of the accident?"

She met his eyes and then looked away. "Honestly? I was more hurt and angry than loving toward him."

"Understandable," he said. And then he saw it: a large elk with a big rack of antlers stood watching them from the woods. "Look," he whispered, tightening his grip on Titan's leash. "No sudden movements."

She turned and sucked in a breath. "So beautiful."

"Yeah," he said, and they watched as the animal nibbled at the skimpy vegetation, having apparently decided they were no threat. It ate grass for a moment, lifted its majestic head as if admiring the view and then loped out of sight.

"Oh, Jason, I'll never forget this moment." She leaned back against him, and he wrapped his arms around her from behind.

Her delight awakened something in him that had long been dormant. He wanted to make her happy. She deserved happiness.

Feeling too much, he loosened his arms, but she surprised him by turning to face him. She looked up, inquiry in her eyes.

He put his hands on her shoulders. "We should go."

"We should." She didn't make a move for the car.

The bright sun warmed his back and put her face into sharp shadow. "Now," he said, not moving, either. "We should go."

She nodded.

Her eyes were wide and her breath made steam in the cold air. A strand of hair blew across her face, and he reached up, pushed it back and tucked it behind her ear. "I've wondered if your hair would be as soft as it looks."

"Is it?" she asked. Her voice was just above a whisper.

He nodded. "It is."

"How about yours?" She reached up and forked her fingers through his hair.

He laughed, trying not to enjoy her tender touch. "Army habit, keeping it short."

"I like it on you."

She liked it on him. Did that mean she liked the way he looked? She was looking at him that way, for sure. And she wasn't moving away.

He put a hand on either side of her face, the lightest touch he could manage. "Do you want me to kiss you?" He'd never done that before, never asked a woman's permission; he hadn't needed to. But with Ashley, with their history, he thought that he should.

She was quiet, although her throat moved, indicating a convulsive swallow.

He let go of her and took a step back. "Hey. It's okay. I shouldn't—"

But she moved forward, closing the gap between them.

She reached up and touched his face, tenderly. “I think… yes. I think I *do* want you to kiss me.”

And at that point, what else could a gentleman do but obey?

Jason’s kiss seemed to go right from Ashley’s lips to her heart, warming her, filling her with giddy happiness.

He kissed like the man he was: strong, masterful, but protective and gentle. He tasted of the sweet peppermint candy they’d shared in the car. Heat shimmered between them and she pushed just a little bit closer, savoring it. Savoring him.

He tugged her into a hug afterward. “I’ve wanted to do that. For…a while.”

She couldn’t admit to the same feelings, even to herself. Instead, she rested her cheek against his chest, listened to his strong, steady heartbeat and felt like she’d finally come home.

She hadn’t, of course.

Later, after an awkward dinner at Jason’s mother and stepfather’s place, Ashley loaded dishes into the dishwasher and washed pots and pans while Jason’s mother sat in a big armchair in the corner of the kitchen. “Thank you for doing that, dear,” the older woman said, her voice weak.

“Of course.” Ashley looked at her former mother-in-law in concern. Marsha was sicker than she’d expected, her skin stretched across her bones, her hair thin. She hadn’t named her illness aloud, although Ashley suspected that was what mother and son had discussed in her bedroom while Ashley and Jason's stepfather had thrown together a simple meal.

Jason had come out looking pale, his mother holding tightly on to his arm. She'd rallied during dinner, but now she looked tired and worn.

Still, she was paying close attention to Ashley, and now she spoke up. "You're wondering why we invited you to come with Jason."

Ashley glanced over at her and nodded, then went back to washing pans, the warm, soapy water soothing her jangled nerves. "I'm curious," she admitted.

"I just wanted to repair the bridges we broke when Christopher died," Marsha explained.

"Of course." There was no point in bringing up the awful things the woman had said in her grief and pain. Especially not now, when she was so sick. "Whatever I can do."

"I wish he were here," Marsha said. "Such a talent, gone."

"He was terrifically talented." That, Ashley could say with sincerity. Christopher had been a brilliant musician.

"And a good husband, too." Marsha studied her. "Wasn't he?"

Did she know something? Ashley's heart rate accelerated. She'd always hidden Christopher's darker side, and what was the point of discussing it now, bringing painful past realities to light?

"He could be very loving," she said, which was true.

Especially after he'd bruised her up.

Jason and his stepfather had been out in the living room watching a game, but now Ashley heard a throat clearing and realized that Jason stood in the doorway,

Titan beside him, listening to their conversation. Heat climbed from her neck to her face as she reviewed what she'd said.

She wanted to keep the past in the past, not reveal it to Jason. She wanted to savor that wonderful kiss they'd shared. To keep it untainted by his brother's ugly behavior.

"There's a box." Mrs. Green tried to stand.

Jason hurried to her side. "Stay here and rest, Mom. I'll get it."

"It's upstairs in the attic," she said. "It's one of those clear plastic boxes and it says 'Christopher' on top."

Ashley finished the cleanup by the time Jason came downstairs with not one but two boxes. "I didn't know which one you wanted, so I brought both," he said.

"Lovely. Pull up chairs, children."

Children?

Was that a joke or was Marsha's mind getting foggy?

Ashley and Jason pulled chairs from the kitchen table to make a circle in front of the older woman, with the two boxes in the middle.

She reached out, and they both leaned forward to grasp hands that felt cold and terribly, terribly frail.

"I may not be around much longer—"

"Mom," Jason interrupted. "We talked about second opinions."

She waved a dismissive hand. "I want to give Christopher's things to the two of you. *He* won't want them," she said, waving a dismissive hand toward the front room to indicate Trent.

That didn't seem right, considering how broken up Trent had been at his son's funeral. Ashley opened her mouth to protest and then closed it again. Marsha knew him better. Maybe keeping his son's things would hurt him rather than help him.

"Do you want us to just take the boxes?" she asked instead.

"No. Let's go through them together and you can each take what you want."

So Jason brought in a low table from the living room and they set the first box on top and opened it.

Awards from Christopher's childhood piano competitions, a Mother's Day craft with a handprint, a few report cards. Ashley's throat tightened. All the mementos a mother would store away, expecting to show them to grandchildren, thinking it would be a happy occasion to look at them again.

Everything changed after a death, of course.

"Oh look, here's a letter he wrote me from music camp," Marsha said, unfolding a piece of paper and spreading it out on her lap. "He was always so loving."

Ashley glanced at Jason, wondering how this was striking him.

But he was looking at his mother with nothing but compassion in his eyes. "He loved you, Mom," he said.

"Of course he did." She raised her eyes, a lone tear rolling down her cheek. "I would never have thought to lose him. But maybe soon we'll be reunited again."

Misery permeated Ashley's bones as they went on through the box, Mrs. Green singing Christopher's praises the whole time.

Of course, he *had* been a wonderful son in some ways, but he'd mostly been neglectful. The cards Mrs. Green had cherished with love, from near the end of Christopher's life, had been chosen by Ashley, and she'd practically had to force Christopher to take a minute to sign them. If he was in a good mood, he'd dash off a line or two.

Finally, they got to the bottom of the first box. Ashley had agreed to take Christopher's awards, while Jason was holding on to the letters and papers. They'd communicated through quick glances. *Just take it—we'll sort it out later.*

That was new, between them, the ability to communicate without words. And Ashley loved it. It was the fruit of their growing connection. The fruit of their kiss.

This, sitting here with Mrs. Green, was painful. But she was Jason's mother, and if Ashley and Jason by some extreme goodness of God built a real relationship, it would matter that Ashley tried to leave the past behind and be kind to her.

"Let's do the other box another day, Mom," Jason said. "I'm sure you're tired. This has to be hard on you."

"No." Her voice was firm. "I want to get this done. Open the other box."

"You're sure you're up to it?" He leaned closer, studying his mother.

"I am."

Ashley couldn't help admiring his kind way with the woman who'd seemed to favor his brother at the best of times and to scapegoat Jason way too often.

Jason lifted the blue plastic lid off the other box and they all peered inside.

Ashley sucked in a breath. The whole box looked to be full of baby clothes, Christopher's clothes.

"I remember him wearing this," Jason said, pulling out a little blue-and-white-checked shirt from the stack of baby clothes.

"Yes, indeed. He looked so cute in it."

Ashley felt like she should say something, like her silence was obvious. But her throat was too tight to push words through it.

"I saved the clothes for Christopher's children," Marsha said, her voice bleak. "I hoped he'd have a son one day."

The sad words pushed and poked and squeezed at Ashley's heart. She pressed her lips together and swallowed hard as images of the baby she'd never know swirled inside her. She had to get out of there before she lost it.

Choking out an excuse, she rushed from the room.

Chapter Nine

Jason looked in the direction Ashley had gone, then turned and looked at Mom, concerned. "Do you think she's okay?" he asked. He could have kicked himself for letting this examination of Christopher's things go on for so long. He'd been so worried about his mother and how she was taking it, given her poor health, that he'd neglected to think about Ashley. She'd had a loss, too, and the past hour—the whole visit, really—had to be bringing it all up again.

If he was being honest, he tended to avoid thoughts of Ashley's marriage to Christopher on purpose. He didn't like thinking about it. Didn't like the mix of guilt and possessiveness that came up when he thought of them together.

Jason looked around the kitchen, trying to get his bearings before deciding whether to go after Ashley or to leave her alone. Surprisingly, the old-fashioned sink with the colorful rug in front of it, the mountain view out the windows and the smell of pie lingering in the air brought back memories, pretty good ones.

He rarely thought of his childhood with fondness. He

didn't remember much before his father had died when he was two. Just a few warm impressions. And then his mom had married Trent and everything had changed. It had changed again after Christopher's birth. But it was worth remembering that they'd had some decent times as a family. Some people had it a lot worse.

Mom was quiet, looking in the direction Ashley had gone, obviously thinking. Finally, she spoke. "Go after her," she said. "Don't ask a lot of questions. Just bring her back here and then leave us alone."

"Why?" He didn't want Mom upsetting Ashley more than she already was.

She closed her eyes for a moment, then opened them and looked at him. "There are a few reasons baby clothes can make a woman cry," she said. "Two of the biggest are that they can't have babies or that they lost a baby."

"Wait—what?" That seemed like a pretty big leap, but what did he know?

"Miscarried," she clarified. "And if either of those is the case—I don't know—she'd do better to talk to someone, another woman, who's been through it."

"Been through it?" He felt foolish echoing her, but he wasn't tracking the conversation well. Did she mean…?

She looked at him for another moment and then nodded in the direction of the door. "Go on."

He didn't move. "When did you…*did* you…lose a baby?"

From the family room, football-game-related shouts came from the TV. Seeking something to do with his hands, Jason broke off a bite of piecrust and crunched into its salty richness.

"It happened several times, over several years." Mom blew out a breath. "Why do you think I got so depressed and withdrawn soon after marrying your stepfather? Why do you think we were so infatuated with Christopher?"

It took a minute, and then what she was saying clicked into place. He remembered his mother taking to her bed, periodically, not to be disturbed. Sleeping a lot, going to the doctor a lot. It had seemed, to his young brain, like Mom had latched on to Trent and then fallen apart.

But maybe something else had been going on. Something that cast a whole new light on the situation. He stood with an assist from Titan, patted his mother's back awkwardly and went after Ashley.

Later, after he'd sat with Trent and watched the last quarter of a game, after a lot of quiet murmuring in the kitchen, Jason heard water running and dishes rattling and even a little laughter. He glanced over at Trent. "Think it's safe to go hunt down another piece of pie?"

"Worth a try."

They both went into the kitchen, Titan following along, to find Mom and Ashley putting out leftovers. Ashley seemed to be keeping her face averted from him. Was she still upset?

Was the reason for it what Mom had suspected? Had Ashley lost a baby?

Both he and Trent got out plates. "After we have a bite, we should leave," Jason said.

"You need to stay over," Mom said firmly. "It's late, and dark." She gave Jason a meaningful look and nodded over at Ashley.

She was carrying something from the refrigerator to the counter. She looked pale, and her eyes were red.

"I don't mind driving," he said, "but we did bring overnight bags in case of weather. I'll leave it up to you, Ash."

Knowing how she'd dreaded coming, he figured she might be eager to leave, but she gave him a tired smile. "I think I'd like to stay and turn in early."

Compassion for her welled up inside him. "Of course. I'll get our bags."

The compassion stayed as he fetched the bags, lifting his face to the cold, snowy wind, thinking.

He'd loved kissing Ashley, but this was something different. This was wanting to take care of her, feeling her emotions as if they were his own.

This was his heart.

That wasn't a good thing, except...maybe it wasn't so impossible as he'd thought.

If she could get along with Mom and Trent... If he himself could get over some of his issues around his childhood... Did they have a chance?

As soon as he came in from the car, he saw Ashley standing in the kitchen doorway, waiting for him.

"You know where to put her bag," Mom said to him with a little catch in her voice.

He nodded and headed upstairs, Ashley following behind. When he set her bag inside the bedroom where she and Christopher had always stayed, he swallowed hard.

Surely she was remembering those times. How could she not? And maybe those times had been filled with a different kind of pain than what he'd thought.

"Look," he said, "I'm sorry things got so emotional. I didn't know that baby clothes would—"

She cut him off with a wave of her hand. "Don't. I can't...not now."

He held his arms open to her, offering comfort. She was free to take it or not. For a moment he thought she'd turn away, and then she stepped forward and laid her cheek against his chest.

In his arms, she felt fragile and birdlike. He held her gently and let her absorb his warmth and his strength. Come what may, he wanted to protect her, care for her.

A few hours ago, he'd been solely absorbed in how good it had felt to kiss her and how forbidden that was, how it couldn't work, how he wasn't good enough. He'd been filled with a mix of excitement and dread that had made him feel a little sick.

But now everything had changed. Now he saw what had made him feel unworthy as a kid in a different light. If Mom had been struggling with all the hormonal issues and grief of miscarriages...if his stepfather had been struggling to manage a new wife and her son, while being unable to have a child of his own... That put a different explanation on some of the ways they'd treated him.

And then Christopher had come along and solved all their problems, and again, Jason had thought it was related to their inherent qualities as people—and it partly was—but really, it had to do with other things. Christopher had been the answer to their prayers for a baby. No wonder they'd treated him like the crown prince.

As for Ashley, if her marriage to Christopher had involved miscarrying a child, then both she and Christopher had been through something more difficult than he'd realized. Wow.

He kissed the top of Ashley's head and turned and left the room before he put his new revelations into some kind of action.

Back at school on Monday, Ashley didn't have time to ponder the emotional visit she'd had with Jason and his family. When she finally emerged from her office at the end of the day, she leaned back against the door in mock exhaustion that wasn't entirely faked. "I thought the weeks between Thanksgiving and Christmas were supposed to be festive and fun," she said to Mrs. Henry.

"Not around here." Mrs. Henry rolled her chair back from her computer. "How'd it go with Flip's parents?"

"I *think* I talked them into leaving him in school." The boy's mother had called to say she wanted Flip to drop out so he could get into a training program for truckers that had opened up in their area. It had been tough to convince her that her son would be better off with a high school diploma and that he *would* have career opportunities afterward.

Mrs. Henry took a phone call and Ashley sank down into one of the office chairs to look through her mail. Not only was she tired from the day, but now that the rush had stopped, she felt how emotionally drained she was.

Telling her mother-in-law about the miscarriage had been a mixed bag. It had been a relief to talk to another woman who'd experienced the same thing, but she hadn't wanted to admit it had happened during the car accident. Hadn't wanted to admit her own culpability and face her mother-in-law's anger and pain.

Letting the woman think that the whole thing had been an act of nature, as her own miscarriages had been, was deceitful, and Ashley didn't feel great about it.

Still, the chance to talk about it, cry about it, with the person who would have been the baby's grandmother had relieved some of her bottled-up feelings.

She tossed the advertisements for educational products and stacked a couple of envelopes to deal with later.

Jason had been so kind at his parents' house, so sensitive to her feelings as they'd driven home.

So wonderful to kiss.

She tried to tell herself she shouldn't focus on that; she should focus on the school. Flip's mother's phone call had served as a reminder about how important it was to offer the boys strong career paths after graduation. That meant that Ashley needed to direct her attention to building up the Young Soldiers program, not to her own foolish romantic dreams.

But the way she'd felt in Jason's arms… He was so strong, yet so tender. She longed to feel that strength and tenderness again, with her whole heart.

She'd just stood when Jason walked into the office.

That square jaw with the slight stubble, the muscles that bulged in his arms, the attentive way he looked at her… She straightened and took a breath. She needed to behave like an adult in charge of a school, not a teenager with a crush.

But it was next to impossible. Titan was with him, and Jason was using his cane today, which she now knew meant he was having a rough time with pain. She also knew now that he didn't like for anyone to comment on it. He wore a denim work shirt, open at the neck, and sturdy, practical pants and work boots, appropriate clothes for his job as a shop teacher, but he somehow managed to look like a model for a rugged men's catalog. That square jaw, those smoky, gold-flecked eyes…

"Isn't that right, Ashley? Ashley?" Mrs. Henry's voice pulled her back into the mundane reality of the school office.

"I'm sorry—what?"

Mrs. Henry raised an eyebrow. "I was telling Jason that we had a tough go-round with Flip's mother today."

Ashley winced at the breaking of a confidence, but then again, Flip's mother had talked loudly to both her and Mrs. Henry about her concerns, and Jason was, after all, one of Flip's teachers.

"I don't know how you stayed patient enough to talk her down," Mrs. Henry said, standing and straightening her desk.

"I talked her down *for now.* It's still touch and go."

"She really wanted to take him out of school in the middle of his senior year?" Jason shook his head.

"I held up the military option. I think that's what calmed her down, for now." She frowned. "Not that there's anything wrong with being a trucker, if that's what he wants, but I'd like to see him finish his high school education."

"He'd have opportunities in transportation and a whole lot more if he enlisted," Jason said. "Plus the chance to see a little more of the world, though..." He grimaced ruefully. "It's not a sightseeing trip. He needs to be on board with the risks as well."

"A boy like Flip might like the risks," Mrs. Henry said. "Well, I'm headed home, even though I still have plenty to do here."

"Go," Ashley said. "Thanks for all your help today."

They both watched Mrs. Henry leave. The outer office door clicked shut behind her. And then it was just the two of them there, looking at each other.

Ashley's mouth went dry.

"Sounds like we should plan another activity for the Young Soldiers," he said. "Besides tomorrow's movie night, I mean. But that's not why I came in."

"Oh?" She brushed a hand over her hair, which was starting to come out of the bun that had been so neat this morning.

"Yeah. This is kind of presumptuous."

He was going to ask her out. How could she respond? She knew it wasn't a good idea. Guilt, slick and uncomfortable, washed over her at the thought that he didn't know how implicated she was in the loss of his brother. Not to mention the nephew he didn't know he could have had, although he had to suspect it after what had happened at his parents' house.

Alongside the guilt, though, was heart-pounding excitement. There was no denying how drawn to him she was.

He reached into his pocket and pulled out a sheaf of folded-in-two papers. "I noticed how upset you were over the weekend. I mean, you know that. But I didn't know quite what to say."

"It's okay." So maybe he *wasn't* going to ask her out? The butterflies in her stomach stopped dancing and started churning and banging around.

He held out the papers. "Since I didn't know the right thing to say, I looked online. I found a good article and printed it out for you."

She took the papers and glanced at the title: "After a Miscarriage: Emotional Healing." Yikes. "That was… thoughtful." She didn't want to talk about the miscarriage with Jason. Didn't want him to know she'd ever had one, actually, but that news was already out.

"You know it's not your fault, right?"

She froze. What did he know?

It *was* her fault, but she didn't want to tell him. Should, but couldn't.

The office clock ticked audible seconds, like every school clock everywhere. A few shouts outside the windows and the sound of a car motor, probably the last staff leaving the parking lot.

Perspiration dripped down her back and her throat felt dry and tight.

She'd chosen the exact wrong moment to tell Christopher of her pregnancy. She, who'd known him better than anyone, known his moods. She'd been a fool. Christopher and their unborn child had paid with their lives.

She leaned a hip against Mrs. Henry's desk as emotions overwhelmed her. *My fault, my fault.*

But she couldn't let herself fall apart.

Young men like Flip needed a strong leader at the helm of the school, someone convinced of the mission's value. She could make the difference in their lives that she'd never be able to make in her child's life.

And she had to stop being foolish, wanting something with Jason that she didn't deserve and could never have.

"Thanks," she said, not looking at Jason, stuffing the papers into her briefcase. "I'd better get back to work. See you later." She turned toward her office.

"Uh…Ashley? Did I do something wrong?"

"I'm really busy right now." She walked into her office. Contemplated slamming the door behind her, but that would be too extreme. Instead, she did the classic half-shut, half-open, "I'm too busy to talk" maneuver.

When she sat at her desk, Jason was still in her line of sight. But totally ignoring him, focusing only on her computer, should get him and Titan out of her hair.

He studied her for another minute; she could feel it, but she didn't look up.

"Right," he said finally. He clicked his tongue to Titan, turned and limped out of the office, not looking back.

So she'd made him angry, or at least hurt. It gutted her, because she really, really wanted to fling herself into his arms.

But the article he'd given her so earnestly had reminded her of the truth: she didn't deserve to be in his arms. Not now. Not ever.

Chapter Ten

"That's a good interpretation." It was the end of movie night, the day after Jason had tried and failed to offer Ashley some concrete help, and he was talking to some of the boys who were still hanging around. Now he stood and held out the last pizza box to Flip and Ethan. "Take this back to your cottage. If you have any more thoughts about the movie, let me know in class tomorrow and we can talk about it."

"Cool." The two boys slouched off, but Jason wasn't fooled by their careless exteriors. They'd paid close attention to the movie, a realistic documentary about life in the service, and they'd been among the most active students in the discussion afterward.

As seniors, they were allowed to walk around campus unsupervised, but Jason still followed them out and watched them head in the direction of the student residences. You couldn't be too careful.

He took a minute for Titan to do his business. Then he faced what he'd been trying to avoid: Ashley, cleaning off the tables and throwing away paper plates and napkins.

They were both headed in the same direction, but would she even walk with him? She'd pushed him away so thoroughly yesterday.

He'd reviewed what he'd said and done. It *had* been presumptuous to give her an article about miscarriages, but he hadn't meant any harm by it. He'd hoped she would find it helpful, hearing how other women coped, seeing the statistics about how many women blamed themselves for miscarriages.

She'd barely glanced at it, though, and then she'd given him clear "go away" vibes.

That was fine. It wasn't as if that one kiss meant anything, right? He'd kissed a lot of women in his day.

But this was different.

It didn't matter that it had felt different to him. It hadn't felt good to her, apparently. Either that or she'd thought better of it. She obviously didn't want to repeat the closeness; she wanted to back off from it.

He needed to focus on what good he could do: help some struggling boys have better lives. That was why he was here. That was his goal as a man, a professional, a Christian.

His brother's widow didn't figure into the equation. Or at least she shouldn't.

He watched her move more and more slowly, and it irritated him. "Look," he said, "you can delay all you want, but I'm not leaving you to walk half a mile by yourself at night. You don't have to talk to me, but you do have to let me walk beside you. Near you, anyway."

She flushed and tossed the paper towel she'd been holding into the trash. "I'm not… Okay, I am. Fine." She grabbed her coat and slipped into it before he could get close enough to help her, not that she'd have let him.

"Ready?" she asked, and hurried out the door ahead of him.

And then she proceeded to walk faster than he could manage, between his cane and Titan. Should he just let her go? Was he really any good to her as a protector when she had more mobility than he did?

She glanced back and slowed down. "I'm sorry. I'm cold."

He started to slip off his coat, but she held up a hand. "No way. I'm not taking your coat. It's like…what, fifteen degrees out?" She blew on her hands.

"Fine." She obviously didn't want any help from him. And maybe she didn't need any, but she sure was shivering. "I'll try to hustle," he said. "Titan, let's go."

The dog was evidently cold, too, because he surged forward. Jason caught his cane on a rock on the icy dirt road and almost went down, but stayed upright with Titan's help.

"I'm sorry. We don't have to rush. Are you okay?"

"I'm good." He walked beside her, but a few feet away, moving as quickly as he dared.

A moment came back to him. A childhood memory of Christopher trying to keep up with Jason. A lot of the time, his half brother had been kept inside, because he had allergies and asthma, and because he had to practice. But on this particular day, he'd tried to tag after Jason, who was headed out for a pickup basketball game with friends.

"Wait up, wait up," Christopher had called, and Jason had waited, but made his annoyance known. "If you don't let me play I'll tell Mom," he'd said as he'd reached Jason, wheezing.

It had rarely been smooth between them. Jason had

been the dominant one outside of the house, with his size and his athletic ability, his ease with other kids. Christopher, though, had been the favored son within the family.

Now Jason thought about that in a new light. If Trent hadn't been able to father a child, he'd probably resented Jason as evidence that Mom's previous husband could. That wasn't sensible, considering that apparently Mom had gotten pregnant several times but had miscarried. But those kinds of emotions weren't often sensible.

It wasn't great if Trent had blamed those adult issues on a kid, but at least it was understandable.

At least it didn't have to do with Jason's unlikability and stupidity, his lack of notable talents, as he'd always thought.

They walked along at a comfortable pace now. Overhead, the sky was dotted with a million stars. So many more than you'd see in a city like Denver. The air, too, was completely pure, filled with pine scent that rivaled anything a Christmas-candle company could produce.

He felt a deep, hungry urge to put an arm around Ashley, pull her closer, keep her warm. Yeah, and more than that; he wanted to kiss her again.

But she'd made it clear she wanted to regain the distance between them, and though he didn't like it, he had to respect it.

He wondered how her marriage with Christopher had been. Before his brother had gotten abusive, had they had at least some warmth and closeness between them?

And then he squashed those thoughts, because he didn't want to know. Didn't want to think of them together.

The last time he'd talked to Christopher, that last

phone call that Jason had happened to make at exactly the right—or the wrong—time, had been ugly. Christopher had thrown out accusations that Jason was involved with Ashley, which was patently ridiculous. Jason had rarely been around them, and never around Ashley alone. He spent holidays with the family and then left as soon as he gracefully could, usually on the same day. No one of sound mind could have thought a man away in the army for that much time could have been involved with his brother's wife.

Besides, Ashley was a loyal wife, loyal to a fault, it sounded like. She'd never given Christopher any cause for jealousy. She'd stuck with him even when he'd become abusive.

Jason would give anything to have saved her from that. The phone call, in fact, had been a failed effort to do just that.

It had backfired because it turned out Christopher was jealous of Jason, had thought there was something between them. There wasn't, but there was a grain of truth in what Christopher had said.

Even though he would never have pursued it, Jason *did* have feelings for Ashley. And the way Christopher treated her, even the little he'd seen, hadn't sat well with him.

That was why he'd made himself scarce during the course of their short marriage.

Now, though… He glanced over at her. Now she wasn't married. Christopher no longer stood between them.

He wanted to know about the accident that had taken Christopher's life. It was something no one discussed, and he'd been overseas at the time. Maybe if they talked about it, they could get past the awkwardness between them. Maybe their relationship would have a chance.

Regardless, he had nothing to lose. "What really caused your car accident?" he asked. It was blunt, maybe rude, but there was never going to be a natural opening for the topic.

She went still for a moment. "You know. The road was icy. And Christopher was driving a little too fast."

"That, I can believe." Christopher had tended to do that, maybe making up for his lack of running speed. He loved fast vehicles and, as his career had prospered, he'd bought several sports cars.

"He was in one of his moods," she said in a hesitant voice. "You know how he could get."

"Yeah." Jason did know. And, moreover, he knew a reason why Christopher might have gotten into that kind of a mood.

Guilt stabbed at him like dozens of tiny, painful knives. If only Jason had handled that phone call better.

"I wish I'd known better how to calm him down," Ashley said, her steps slowing.

"Are you kidding? You were great at that! You were the only one who *could* calm him down."

"Not always," she said, shaking her head. "Not that night."

She looked up to the clouds, blew out a sigh and picked up the pace again.

The wind felt colder now, the stars more distant. Jason tried to push away the past, tried to ignore his brother's almost palpable presence, but it was impossible.

Christopher was here, and he'd always be between them. There wasn't going to be a relationship with Ashley.

Because now Jason was even more sure that his phone call had contributed to Christopher's death.

"All aboard the Christmas Train!" Ashley called as she adjusted her Santa Claus hat and jingled her leather strap of bells. It was Saturday afternoon, and most of the Bright Tomorrows boys were here at the Little Mesa train station. Their scenic train ride included an hour through the mountains, a stop at the nearby town of Merry Creek and a return trip before dark.

Ashley wasn't the only one dressed up. Since they had so many boys in attendance, a number of staffers had come along, and most wore reindeer antlers or had bells around their necks. Hayley was dressed all in green, as a Christmas elf. Even Jason wore an ugly Christmas sweater with a colorful Christmas tree that actually lit up—she hadn't known they made such things in his size—and he'd put a holiday kerchief on Titan. They were following, or herding, a group of students onto the train.

"I'm so glad we're doing this," Hayley said as they climbed aboard the cheerfully decorated train after making sure no students had been left behind on the platform. "We can sit together, right? Or do you want us to split up to supervise?"

"We can sit together. Nobody wants to sit with the principal, that's for sure." Including Jason, but she wasn't going to think about him today. The closeness they'd shared when they'd kissed had gotten further and further away every time they talked about Christopher and the way things had ended up. Even if they were able to regain some kind of friendship, it could never be close as long as they couldn't be open about that.

Today, she was going to focus on the students, help them to enjoy the day, give them a good Christmas memory.

They found seats at the back of one of the train cars, where they could watch everything that was going on. The worn upholstery and old-fashioned windows showed that this was a real train, not something created new for Christmas events. But to Ashley, that made it better. There was tinsel woven through the baggage racks and the conductor wore a red bow tie and joked with everyone as he checked their tickets. Christmas music played through the speakers.

The train started moving, jerky at first, and then smoother as they picked up speed.

"This is going to be fun!" Hayley bounced a little in her seat.

"You may be the only one who thinks so." Some of the older boys had already expressed their opinion that the whole activity was way too childish for them, and the younger boys had mostly followed suit, not wanting to seem uncool. Ashley just hoped that they'd catch the Christmas spirit soon and enjoy the day.

"I think they'll get caught up in it," Hayley said. "I mean, look at that!" A golden retriever wearing a red coat with a small stuffed Santa riding on its back trotted through the aisle, released by the conductor at the front and running to a Christmas elf in back. Sure enough, most of the boys at least leaned out to watch, and several smiled and laughed at the sight. Ashley was happy to see Langston Murray, the boy who'd gotten so upset in Jason's class, reach out a hand to touch the dog as it went by. He was sitting by one of the other boys from the school and they were talking and laughing. He was settling in, it seemed.

There were other people in the car unconnected with the school; families with little ones who yelled and bounced and reached out to the dog as it ran by.

Ashley nodded. "I *hope* the boys like it. For some of them, Christmas stuff like this is nostalgia from their childhoods. Others never had this type of activity before. Either way, it's a good thing." She looked over at Ethan and Flip, seated across the aisle and a row ahead. Ethan was on his phone, and Flip was reading a thick paperback with a gory cover. She sighed. "Maybe. Maybe it's a good thing."

"It'll be great." Hayley settled back in her seat. "I mean, just a train ride through the mountains is a treat."

"Don't get too comfortable," Ashley warned. "I want the boys to have a special activity, but I also want to get some cute photos for our website and social media." That was another effort she was making: to update their site and improve their online image. She hoped it would pay off in a few new students at least.

"I'll keep an eye out," Hayley promised, waving her phone. She was a much better photographer than Ashley was.

Hayley started talking to the boys across the aisle, and Ashley sat back and looked out the window. Sparkling white snow, deep green pine trees, and blue sky overhead: pure Colorado. You couldn't look around without seeing God's handiwork everywhere.

A bigger perspective, too. Those mountains had been there long before Ashley had been born, and they would outlast her. Generations of people had ridden this very train route, had come and gone, and the mountains remained.

It put her problems with the school, and with Jason, into perspective. She leaned her head back and let the joy of the season, the peace of God, envelop her.

She must have dozed off, but she jerked awake to the sound of boys laughing and talking. Hayley smiled at her. "I'm glad you woke up. Check it out," she said.

Two cute teen girls, their short red dresses trimmed with white fur, were talking to Flip and Ethan. They seemed to be employees rather than guests, because they wore name tags and carried official Christmas Train bags, but clearly their duties weren't onerous. They didn't seem to be in any hurry. One lounged on the seat arm across the aisle, and one leaned on the seat-back in front of the boys.

"The older boys like the train now, huh?" she asked sleepily.

"Yes, and so do the other boys." Hayley gestured around the train car, where the sound of laughter and even some carol singing could be heard.

One of the teen girls pulled two striped stocking caps from her bag and presented them to Flip and Ethan. The two boys looked at each other, shrugged and put the caps on.

"Photo op," Hayley called, and hurried up the aisle to take pictures: of the two boys alone, then with the girls, and then of other boys.

When she came back, Ashley thanked her. "You're the best. Send me those, or just post them yourself. You have the list, right?" There were certain boys who weren't to be photographed, per their parents' or guardians' instructions.

"On it," Hayley promised as she slid her phone into her pocket and settled in her seat. "So what's up with you and Mr. Cranky?"

"Who?" Ashley asked, although she could guess.

Hayley nodded toward the front corner of the car, where Jason sat, alone except for Titan. It was a sideways seat, probably originally meant for riders with disabilities. Maybe those seats still served that function. Ashley couldn't see from here, but she assumed he'd sat there so there'd be room for Titan.

Ashley hadn't seen him come into this car, and now she studied his face. It wasn't tight with pain, like sometimes, but Hayley was right: the corners of his mouth were turned down, and he wasn't interacting with the boys the way he normally would have.

Hayley nudged her again. "So? Spill it. What's going on with you two?"

"Nothing." Ashley glanced around the train car, checking on the boys and also making sure Hayley's questions couldn't be overheard.

But the boys were all talking and laughing, well occupied. Good. The last thing she needed was for gossip to start happening around her relationship with Jason. She could almost hear the Captain's views on *that*.

"You spent Thanksgiving together, and you've planned the entire Young Soldiers program together, and...*nothing* is happening?"

"We have a professional relationship," Ashley said. She was trying to sound uninterested in the topic, but her cheeks flamed with heat.

Hayley was studying her. "I don't buy that," she said. "I think something's going on."

Ashley waved a dismissive hand. "It's nothing."

"Give!" Hayley insisted.

"Shh!" Ashley glanced around again. "It's not going anywhere. We kissed, but it was a mistake," she said in a near whisper.

Hayley's jaw dropped and then she fist-bumped Ashley. "Why isn't it going anywhere?"

Because I hurt his feelings on purpose, so he wouldn't find out the truth about the nephew he might have had.

She shrugged and shook her head, looking away from Hayley's insightful gaze. The memory of that kiss would stay with her, and she couldn't help but regret what could have been. What would it be like if they didn't have a past, if they'd met all clean and new, if they were sitting together right now, watching the boys warm up to the childlike joy of Christmas?

It would be beautiful, but Ashley couldn't let herself wallow in that.

"Ho ho ho!" The deep, booming laugh came from the front of the car as Santa walked through, giving candy to the kids. Santa paused by Ricky's seat and spoke to the helper elf behind him. Then he knelt.

"What's he doing?" Ashley couldn't tell from her seat by the window.

"He's signing Ricky's cast! And Ricky looks so thrilled." Hayley stood to get a better angle and snapped photos.

The teen girls were still hanging around Flip and Ethan, and they clapped and called to Santa, who gave them and the boys big handfuls of candy. Hayley snapped pictures of the older boys' smiling faces, and Ashley looked around the car.

Even the quieter boys looked happy and enthusiastic.

In the front of the car, Dev had sat next to Jason, and the two men were talking.

The mountains flew past and, finally, the train slowed. They must be near their destination.

All of a sudden, a woman unassociated with the school stood and looked around herself, her face distressed. Soon her two little girls were looking around, too, and other nearby passengers got involved as the train came to a halt.

The bow-tied conductor stopped and spoke to her.

The woman straightened. "My purse is missing," she said, glaring at the three Bright Tomorrows boys closest to her. Ricky, Flip and Ethan. "And one of *you* stole it!"

Chapter Eleven

Jason was on his feet and moving toward the commotion in seconds, the sudden movement wrenching his back painfully.

"I heard you talking," the red-faced woman shouted at Flip, Ethan and Ricky. "You're from a school for delinquents!"

Jason narrowed his eyes and moved faster. This unpleasant woman could stir up some real trouble.

Ashley squeezed her way past Hayley, who seemed to be videoing the scene. "Ma'am. Slow down," she said in a calming voice that appeared to have no effect whatsoever.

But since Ashley was focused on the woman, Jason focused on the boys. "Hey, it's okay," he said to Ricky, who looked to be near tears. "I know you didn't do it."

"How do you know?" the woman screeched, turning to him. She saw Titan, directly behind him, and her lip curled. "And why is that enormous dog allowed on a train? My girls are terrified of dogs!"

On cue, the pink-clad twins began to cry.

Jason put a hand on Ricky's shoulder and looked past

him to Ethan and Flip, his real worries. He'd taken this job so he could help troubled boys, and here was where the rubber hit the road. They were being stereotyped and scapegoated, and Jason knew the feeling all too well. Every bad thing that had happened in his family had been blamed on him, and it had made him live down to other people's low expectations.

The boys had been muttering, but as the woman's accusations continued to mount, they started to talk back. Mouths curled, fists clenched, and they actually began to look more like bad, troublemaking kids. They were becoming what the woman accused them of being.

"I'm calling the police," she cried. She held up her phone. "See, I'm calling 9-1-1 right now."

Her girls' wails got louder. The place was turning into a zoo. Out the window, Jason could see that most of the staff, the Santa and the conductor were helping people off the train.

Ashley's voice had cooled, gone all-principal, and she'd drawn herself up, straightening her shoulders. She stepped between the woman and the teen boys, fearless.

His goal for the day had been to keep his distance from Ashley as he focused on the boys, but how could he do that with this drama unfolding in front of him?

He'd lost track of Ricky, but now the boy clambered out into the aisle, cast and all. "Your purse is under your seat, lady," he said, pointing.

She grabbed it. "You probably stole it and put it back."

Jason cleared his throat. "I think an apology is in order."

"That's right," the lady said, looking expectantly at the boys.

"I mean from you. You made some pretty ridiculous assumptions and you've been extremely rude."

The woman looked shocked and she reached down for her little girls, pulling them against her, trying to cover their ears. "How dare you say such things in front of my children!"

"You didn't have a problem screaming false accusations in front of them and everyone else in the train car. Are you thinking you're a good role model?"

Ashley reached past the woman and put a hand on his arm. His mouth had been open to say more, but he closed it.

"The show's over," she said to the boys who remained, watching. "Let's get back to enjoying the season." Her voice was calm, but steely.

Hayley started urging the boys off the train and, after a minute, Jason did, too, staying behind himself. He could hear Ashley speaking with the woman, the little girls' wails subsiding.

Once the car was nearly empty, the woman pushed past Jason, clearly in a huff. Titan gave a little yelp.

"Mommy, you stepped on his toe," one of the girls said.

"He's in the way. Come on." She marched to the exit, pulling her daughters behind her.

Jason sat on the edge of a seat and checked Titan's massive paw, taking deep breaths to keep himself from chasing after the woman and strangling her.

"Is he okay?" Ashley sat on the edge of a seat, too, across the aisle and one row up.

Jason glanced around and saw that they were the only

people remaining in the train car. He pressed gently on the dog's foot, eyeing him closely. "I'm watching for a reaction," he explained, looking up at Ashley and then back at the dog. "Titan's pretty stoic. If he gets hurt, he tends to mask it."

"She must have stepped on him hard to make him yelp like that." She reached out a hand, hesitantly, and Titan stepped toward her, then leaned against her, his way of encouraging her to rub his head and ears.

Ashley obliged. "You poor baby," she crooned.

That was progress. "I thought you were afraid of him."

"I am, a little," she said. "But I like him, too." She was rubbing both of Titan's ears now, looking into his eyes. "You showed a lot of restraint, didn't you, boy? If I had teeth like yours, I might have taken a bite out of that lady."

Jason had examined all four paws now and hadn't detected a reaction. He'd also seen Titan walk without limping as he'd moved closer to Ashley. "I think he's okay," he said, "though I'll keep an eye on him."

"I guess we should get out there," Ashley said, but rather than moving, she turned fully into her seat and leaned back against the headrest.

Jason looked out the window. "I think Hayley and Dev are herding everyone toward the shops."

"That's good." She let out a sigh. "Thanks for coming to the boys' defense."

"Same to you. You were a lot calmer."

"It took a village to defuse that." She drew in a big breath and let it out in a sigh. "Hayley filmed everything, so if there are police ramifications, we'll have that at least."

"As well as a lot of eyewitnesses. Not all of them from the, quote, 'school for delinquents.'" There had been several other civilian families on the train, and from their expressions as they'd herded their kids away from the argument and off the train, Jason was pretty sure they'd realized how unreasonable the woman was being.

He took some deep breaths himself, bringing his heart rate down to normal, petting Titan. He'd tried his best to keep a distance from Ashley after their stilted conversation Tuesday night, but he'd been hyperaware of her all week and especially during the train ride.

He stood, a little awkwardly. "Wrenched my back a little," he said, smiling at her.

"I'm sorry about that, but I can't be sorry you came to their defense. It meant a lot." She stood, too, and gathered her things.

"I got a little hot under the collar. Probably shouldn't have criticized her in front of her kids, when it comes to that."

She looked at him and held his eyes. "No. I was watching the boys, and they calmed down as soon as you started reading her the riot act. Most of them don't have much experience having someone take their side."

Their gazes tangled and Jason's heart swelled. She was looking at him with pride and admiration.

Exactly the way a husband would want his wife to look at him.

What a thought.

They walked off the train and into a Christmas wonderland. Up here, everything was snow-covered, and the shop windows were fully decorated with lights and trees and animated figures.

"Do you smell chocolate?" Ashley asked.

He sniffed the air and looked around. There was a shop with a candy-cane-striped awning. "Sure do, and it's coming from that fudge shop. Can I buy you a piece?" As soon as he said it, he regretted it. That was a dating thing to say, a boyfriend thing to say.

Not a late husband's brother thing to say.

She looked at him for a minute, speculatively. "Let's make sure the boys are doing okay, and then yes. You can."

It was wrong, but his heart swelled with pleasure. He just had to remember nothing could come of it.

So they walked the length of the block and through the barn that was full of activities: old-fashioned ring toss and hoop games, colorful crafts and, of course, a photo booth. Ethan and Flip were posing there with the teen girls. "Looks like they're happy again," Ashley said. "Although I'll be sure and talk to each of the boys involved, see how they're handling being accused like that."

"Good idea. If they're anything like me, they're used to stuffing down their feelings. Especially when there are pretty girls around to impress."

She raised an eyebrow at him but didn't say anything. She was thinking it, though, so he blurted out, "Yes, I consider you a pretty girl, if I can say that about my boss. And I probably hide a few not-nice feelings when you're around, but that's a good thing."

Two pink spots appeared on her cheeks. Great, now he'd upset her. What he'd said had been totally inappropriate. What he *felt* was totally inappropriate.

Ethan had an arm around one of the red-clad elves. Almost glad for the distraction from his mixed-up emotions, Jason narrowed his eyes, wondering if he ought to intervene. But the Mrs. Claus who was taking the pictures came over and tugged the girls into some activity.

Situation resolved.

If only he could resolve his own feelings, or his own history. Stop blaming himself for his role in his brother's car accident. If only he could make her laugh and get a picture taken of the two of them together. If only they could ride home on the train holding hands.

But he couldn't. That wasn't going to happen.

So, for now, he'd have to content himself with being near her and buying her a big bag of chocolate.

Ashley walked out of church on Sunday feeling a little bit hopeful. The train ride yesterday had been a near disaster, but in the end things had turned out okay.

She'd spoken with two of the three boys affected, and they'd definitely been hurt by what the woman on the train had said. She'd talked with them about how other people's views of you didn't represent the truth, necessarily, and how important it was not to take things personally. That, combined with conversations they'd apparently had with Jason, had seemed to help them process the experience and learn from it.

She needed to touch base with Flip, who was keeping to himself more than she'd like to see. And she was also on the lookout for any negative gossip in town or, worse, online or in the media.

So that was stressful—she couldn't deny it. But what she also couldn't deny was that the experience had tugged her closer to Jason again.

She'd admired how he'd stood up for the boys, how his automatic urge was to protect them. He believed in them and was loyal; it hadn't even occurred to him—

any more than it had to Ashley—that there was a chance one of them had taken the purse. That had made an enormous difference to the boys.

Afterward, processing all of it with him, she'd felt close, understanding, understood. And she'd also felt a gazillion sparks between them. The way their gazes kept tangling, the way it had felt when their hands had accidentally touched… She got a funny tingle in her stomach just thinking about it.

It needed to stop. She couldn't kiss him again, couldn't even go in that direction. Not with the unhappy history they shared.

The words of Pastor Nate's sermon today echoed in her mind: *forgive as you have been forgiven*. He'd stressed that forgiveness needed to be applied to one-self, too, that being self-punishing about something in the past, something Christ had already forgiven you for, was almost an insult to God.

She'd never thought about it that way before, but maybe, just maybe, she needed to stop beating up on herself about the accident. She'd made mistakes, terrible ones, but to continue whipping herself for it… Did that do any good, really?

She walked out into the cold sunshine, breathed in the icy air and looked around for her group. Pastor Nate had asked for volunteers to visit and help decorate a local nursing home, and Ashley had decided to go. It was something she'd done last year as well, and found it a meaningful way to celebrate the Christmas season, as well as being just plain fun.

Jason had been at the service. He'd heard the request for more volunteers.

Would *he* be going?

She saw him headed for his car, Titan at his side, and fell into step beside him. After all, their cars were parked in the same part of the lot.

He smiled over at her. The man had a seriously good smile.

"What's up?" he asked. "You headed home?"

"Going to the nursing home." She swallowed. "Are you planning to come?"

He tilted his head to one side and studied her, and she could read his question as clearly as if he'd said it aloud. *Are you inviting me?*

She kind of was, but she shouldn't. Partly to avoid setting up expectations that couldn't be fulfilled. And partly because, if he said no, it would hurt.

Still, she'd opened that door and she had to say something. "There are a lot of veterans at the nursing home," she said, her words tumbling over each other. "Maybe we can figure out a service activity the boys could do with them. But don't feel like you have to come."

He was still studying her, almost as if he were trying to read beneath the words she was saying.

"I mean, you work enough during the week, and you came along yesterday—"

He touched her arm and a sparkler lit inside her, stopping her words. "Ashley," he said. "It's okay. I'd like to come."

Half an hour later, she was untangling strings of lights while Jason and a couple of other men from the church brought out boxes of artificial Christmas trees. The nursing home had three rooms that needed to be decorated: the common room, the dining room and a craft room.

The men set the Christmas tree boxes in each of the rooms and then divided the task of putting them up.

When Jason offered to take charge of the trees in the common room, putting him on a team with Ashley, butterflies fluttered in her chest.

She was worse than the teenagers who were hanging around the room, visiting with the five or six residents who sat watching and commenting on all the activity. They were more attuned to the reason for the activity than she was.

She refocused on her work, stretching out strings of lights. Jason called Flip over—he'd been reading a paperback thriller in the corner of the room—and got him to assist with putting trees together. Good. Maybe they could spend time talking about what had happened yesterday.

She'd been surprised to see Flip and Ethan here, but they did attend church in town, along with a number of other boys from the school, and apparently a van full of teens had joined the decorating crew. That wasn't the kind of thing those particular two usually volunteered to do, and Ashley was fine with that; the boys had to behave all week in school, and they deserved to nap or play video games or do whatever other recreation they enjoyed on a Sunday.

When a group of girls from town arrived, dressed in matching short, fur-trimmed red dresses and striped tights, it all started to make more sense. Especially when she recognized the two girls from yesterday's train ride.

Flip gamely helped Jason put three trees together, and then he headed off to talk to the other teens. Jason came over to Ashley. "Ready to string some lights?" he asked.

"Sure." Her heart thumped faster in her chest, making it hard to breathe.

He reached for the tip of the string, and their fingers touched, and Ashley's face heated. She glanced at him and their gazes tangled.

Whoa. They were in a nursing home with elders and teens. There was no call for *that* type of feeling. "If you can sort of twist these around the top, we'll string them back and forth down the front."

"You're not a 360-degree light stringer?" he asked. "Funny, I'd have pegged you for that."

"What?" She looked at him.

His expression was teasing. "Don't you know that's an even bigger controversy than whether to have white or colored lights? There are people who think you should spiral the lights all around the tree, front and back. And then there are those who think you should zigzag back and forth across the front and leave the back undecorated."

She smiled at that. "How do you know so much about the philosophy of tree decorating?"

"Because Mom and Trent got into it every year. She was a stickler for the 360-degree spiral, while he was more about putting the lights all up front." As he spoke, he was tucking the first strand of lights around the top of the artificial tree.

She took up the job, stretching the lights partway around the tree and then zigzagging them back when she reached the corner of the room, stretching them across the front of the tree. That meant she had to duck underneath Jason's extended arm. Brush past his sweater, feeling the soft wool of it on her arm. Smell his slight scent, a mix of outdoor pine air and some fresh, bright soap. Feel the heat that radiated from him.

Right. Because he was a heat machine; he'd told her that himself.

Her own insides warmed and she sidled to the other side of the tree. "Which did you agree with?"

He laughed; a deep, resonant sound that seemed to vibrate through her. "I learned pretty early that it was best to agree with Mom and do what she said. Chris, though, he'd always get into the fight."

That sounded like Christopher, and the thought of him cooled the heat that had risen in her.

The teens were unwrapping ornaments and their conversation had gotten loud. Ashley was glad to focus on that instead of her complicated feelings for the man beside her. "Wonder if we should tell them to tone it down?" She brought the strand back, and this time, he gave her a quick glance and then stepped away from the tree so she could get through.

"I'm keeping an eye on them. I'm glad I came. They're a handful."

She raised an eyebrow. "You think you can handle them better than I can?"

He snorted. "No. You have way more experience. But if you have to drag one of them away and scold him, I can supervise the others."

The voices rose louder still, two in particular: Flip and Ethan, who stood glaring at each other. "Shut up," Flip said to his friend, who currently looked like more of an enemy.

A couple of the staffers looked concerned. Most of the elders were ignoring the teens—here was where age-related hearing loss came in handy—but Ashley definitely didn't want to let things accelerate. Another public altercation this weekend would be a bad thing for the school.

Ashley dropped the string of lights and headed over, Jason beside her, Titan at his side.

Flip was right up in Ethan's face. The possibility that they'd come to blows was suddenly real.

Jason waded in between them. His hands were at his sides, he wasn't being threatening, but the bulk of him had the effect of separating the boys.

Ashley skimmed her eyes over the situation and settled on one of the girls who was watching, arms crossed, a little smile on her face.

She cut that girl off from the others like a predator separating one piece of prey from the flock. "What's going on?" she asked the girl, nodding back at the two boys. "You're Amanda, right?"

"Yeah. I'm not sure. They just started arguing," she said.

Ashley sensed there was more to the story, but this girl wasn't her responsibility, so she couldn't push it. She did see, though, as Flip and Ethan glared at each other and snapped answers to Jason's questions, that having an audience wasn't doing the situation any good.

She shifted her attention to all three girls. "Could you take over putting the lights on that tree? And then the ornaments are in the boxes stacked by the door. Make it look as good as you can." She thought of a way to sweeten the deal. Teen girls, especially, loved photo ops. "I think we're going to take some pictures there after."

"Sure," one of the girls said, and they immediately went over to do the job.

"Could we talk about this in the break room?" she

asked, putting one hand on Jason's arm and the other on Flip's. "We're upsetting the residents."

All three glanced over at the small crowd of elders. They actually didn't look all that upset, but still, the sharp tension had been broken.

"Cookies..." Ashley said, trailing off and smiling. Making things lighter still, plus the way to a man's heart...

"Fine." Flip stomped in that direction, and Jason went after him.

"You, too," Ashley said, and urged Ethan to come along.

In the break room, a plate of frosted sugar cookies sprinkled with red sugar helped to de-escalate the situation a little more. Still, it seemed prudent to put the two boys on opposite sides of the table.

"So...anyone want to tell me what's going on?" Ashley asked. Then she bit into a sugar cookie. "Oh wow, so good."

All three males instantly grabbed another cookie, but it was Jason's eyes that lingered on her.

Self-conscious, she brushed a little sugar from the side of her face.

Neither boy spoke up, so Jason did. "Apparently, they've both been texting the same girl, thinking they were the only one. And now they're fighting."

"Amanda?"

"Yeah," Flip said.

Ethan nodded. "She likes me, and he's bugging her."

"That's not true! She said she'd go out with me over the break."

"She told me that, too!" Ethan stood and leaned over the table, almost upending the plate of cookies.

"Hey! Careful!" Flip straightened the cookies and shoved them out of reach. "I talked to her first. She's mine."

"Well, I texted her first," Ethan countered, looming closer to the other boy.

Flip started to stand.

"Okay, okay, wait a minute. Sit down, Ethan." By using her "principal" voice, she got compliance, though the two boys still glared at each other. "First of all, she's not like a coin you found on the sidewalk, finders keepers. She's a human being."

"Truth." Jason took another sugar cookie and then shoved the plate back toward the boys, winking at Ashley.

He was actually enjoying this! She narrowed her eyes in a mock glare.

"Besides that," she said, refocusing on the boys, "is she really worth ruining a friendship of…what, five years? You two have been like brothers."

Something flashed across Jason's face. She only saw it out of the corner of her eye, but she knew immediately what he was thinking.

Some brothers, like him and Christopher, *weren't* close.

Weird how good she was becoming at reading his mind.

The two boys were still frowning, looking mad, but at least they weren't in each other's face.

"I'm not sure I should say this, but…do you think Amanda was kind of enjoying all this? Because that was my impression."

"Touché," Jason said. "Some women—some *people*—enjoy setting up fights between other people."

"And some people like attention," Ashley said.

"Yeah." Ethan nodded. "She *is* kind of that type."

Then everyone looked at Flip.

"You know," he said finally, "she was texting both of us, making promises and acting like she liked us a lot."

"She was probably just playing us."

"That's—"

Jason held up a hand, halting the language that was surely about to come out of Flip's mouth. "So she's not worth fighting over," he said. "But also, a gentleman doesn't speak harshly to a lady. Even if you're mad at her, take it out in the gym or go for a run."

How had Jason's brother, Christopher, missed *that* memo?

"You can dump her," Jason went on, "but do it politely. Preferably in person."

That sounded like pushing it. "If your friendship mostly happened by text, though, you can break up that way as well."

"I'm texting that—" Flip broke off. "That young lady," he said, flashing a grin at Ashley and Jason.

She fist-bumped him. "Perfect."

"Me, too." Ethan was on his phone, typing away.

"Well done, men," Jason said. "Can you two do that without killing each other?"

Flip glanced up. "If you leave the cookies," he said.

"Deal." Ashley looked at Jason and nodded sideways at the door. "Our work here is done."

Jason snapped his fingers, and Titan lumbered to his feet. They all strolled back out to the common room, where it looked like, between the church people, the girls and the seniors, the work was nearly done.

On the threshold, Jason touched her arm. "You were great in there," he said.

"As were you." She smiled up at him, and then they both seemed to have the same idea, sidestepping to the back of the room to watch the proceedings. "I'm glad you thought to tell them not to take out their feelings on Amanda."

"Life lessons," he said. "Believe me, I've felt the way they feel before."

Ashley opened her mouth to respond, and then she processed what he'd said. "You mean...you've felt, like... jealous over a woman?"

He leaned against the wall and crossed his arms over his chest. "Don't play dumb."

"I'm not. I mean, I would have expected you to have a dating history, but I didn't know jealousy was involved."

"Ashley. Think."

Understanding of his implication dawned on her. She leaned back, too, but didn't look at him. "I don't know what to say. Are you talking about me and Christopher?"

He hesitated. "I don't feel great about admitting it, but I was jealous. I was...drawn to you."

Ashley's face heated. "For how long?"

He lifted one shoulder and kept his eyes trained on the activities at the other end of the room. "Since I met you. That's why I kept my distance."

Ashley didn't know what to say. Heat suffused her whole body to think of that. She'd always noticed that Jason had been a little standoffish with her, had felt that, maybe, he didn't even like her that much. But if his distance had come from another reason... "You never said anything. To me, at least. Not to..." She frowned as things shifted into a different light. "You didn't speak to Christopher about it, did you?"

"No. And I would never have acted on it. Even back then, when I was maybe not the best person in the world. But he..." Jason trailed off.

"But he knew," she finished.

"I think so, yeah. In fact, I know so, but how do *you* know?"

"Because when he was angry with me, Christopher talked like he was jealous of *you*. He accused me of being attracted to you."

"Whoa." Jason glanced over at her and then back out at the roomful of people.

"It got worse as time went on. Especially after that one time when you—" She broke off.

"Yeah," he said.

She sucked in a breath and said what had to be said. "I just want you to know I never gave him cause to worry about me that way. I never looked at another man when I was married to him."

And that was true. If she'd noticed anything about Jason, it wasn't on a conscious level.

But Christopher had sensed something, or he'd thought he had, and it was one of the things he'd yelled at her during their last awful fight in the car.

Should she tell him about what Christopher had said? She looked over at him. His jaw was clenched, and it almost seemed a symbol of how rigidly he held himself in control. Knowing what Christopher thought he'd done... No. He didn't need to be burdened with that.

He reached a hand down to Titan. "I'm going to go check on the boys," he said. His tone was curt. He turned and walked away.

So…once again they'd started to have a good conversation, they'd worked together, and she'd felt close… and then, abruptly, he'd pulled back and disappeared.

She shouldn't feel disappointed about that, but she did.

Chapter Twelve

Jason walked away from Ashley, fast, Titan at his side. He'd come to the nursing home at her invitation, to help her plan an activity with the veterans, but that wasn't going to work out.

With half a mind, he noticed the half-decorated Christmas trees, the few residents who were helping the church people and teenagers with the decorating, the carols playing in the background while people talked and laughed together.

He would plan an activity with the veterans himself or, better yet, with the boys. That was his responsibility.

Ashley wasn't.

He recognized his own slight feeling of hostility toward her: it was guilt, pure and simple. He felt more implicated than ever when he thought about the phone call he'd made to Christopher on that fatal last day of his life.

He'd already felt awful about the timing of it, the note he and his brother had ended on. It was true that they hadn't been close, that they'd been more different than alike, but despite that, they were brothers. Half brothers, but they'd grown up together since Jason was a kid and Christopher was born.

That phone call and what Jason had said had infuriated Christopher, scratched the scab off a wound. Had Jason let his feelings for Ashley show? Had his words pushed his brother into having a wreck?

He shook off the memories and spoke to an aide who was standing to the side, watching the bustle in the room. "I'd like to talk to a couple of your veterans, see about planning an activity with some of the boys from Bright Tomorrows," he said. "Is there anyone you'd recommend who might like to brainstorm with us?"

The aide looked around. "Ralph would be good. Freddy, too. Want to meet up with them in the activity room?" He pointed down the hall.

"Sure. I'll round up a couple of my boys."

His boys. When had he started to think of them that way?

He looked around for Flip and Ethan and found them sitting on opposite ends of a couch, looking at their phones. "Hey, guys. I need you to help me with something. Over in the activity room." He glanced in Ashley's direction. She was talking with a couple of the residents, not looking his way.

Good. He was probably wrong to start planning something without her, but he couldn't deal with her right now.

He ascertained that the boys were actually moving and then hurried up toward the activity room, not wanting Ashley to notice and check on what he was doing.

As he turned the corner, his back went out.

He couldn't restrain an exclamation as pain radiated

from his injury site up and down his spine. He grabbed for Titan as he went down hard onto his knees.

He tried to hold himself perfectly still, knowing from experience that the pain would be excruciating when he started moving. Inwardly, he berated himself. This was residue from yesterday's exertion.

He leaned heavily on Titan, grateful for the big dog's muscular frame and steady, sturdy stance. Behind him, people were still talking and laughing. Hopefully that meant people hadn't noticed his fall. But getting up was going to be an issue.

"Hey, Mr. Smith, you okay?" Ethan asked, coming to his side.

"No, he's not okay. He fell!" Flip knelt beside him. "Want us to pull you up?"

"Yeah. But slow and careful." He held out an arm to Flip, and then let go of Titan and reached for Ethan. The two boys pulled and he got his feet under him, clenching his jaw to keep from yelling. Once he was steady, he let go of the boys and held on to Titan again.

"You need one of the nurses?" Flip asked.

"Or Ashley?"

"No. Just…go…ahead. Room's on…the right." He nodded in the direction of the activity room, and the boys looked doubtfully at him and then headed for it.

Jason followed, slowly, each step agonizing. At the doorway, he looked back toward the common room. He could only see a slice of it, but the action was still going on with no disturbance. Good. No one had noticed his fall.

Especially Ashley. He knew her well enough to figure out that she'd fuss over him. No matter that he'd been rude to her, if he was in need, she'd drop any feelings against him and come to his aid. That was who she was.

He made his way into the room and lowered himself into a wide, sturdy chair. He couldn't stop himself from wincing.

"Are you sure you're okay, Mr. Smith?" Ethan's expression was concerned.

The nurse who'd wheeled one of the veterans in was looking at him, and so were the two vets. "Fine," he gritted out.

"Ring if you need anything," the nurse said, and walked out after a doubtful glance at Jason.

One of the veterans, his long hair in a braid, was in a wheelchair, while the other wore a ball cap and sat on a regular chair. They, and the two boys, looked at him expectantly.

He tried to explain. "Thanks for meeting…with us." He sucked in a deep breath and let it out slowly. His back throbbed and cramped. "We—they—would like to do…a service project with the…veterans here." He was out of breath from speaking through the intense pain.

"We can talk about that, son," the long-haired vet replied, "but looks like you might need to see a doctor first."

"No…it's just…my back."

The two veterans looked at each other. "You need to stay on top of that pain," the guy with the ball cap said. "Do you have meds?"

"Yeah," Jason grumbled. And he'd love to take a couple of pain pills. "Try to keep them for the real serious pain."

"This isn't serious pain?" Flip asked.

"Don't be a hero. Take something for it." The long-haired man wheeled closer. "You sure I can't get you a doctor?"

"Where are your pills?" the other man asked, coming over, too.

Jason shook his head and shifted in his seat, the movement so painful that he lost his breath. "Can't. Driving home."

"I have my license," Flip said. "I can drive you home in your car."

"No. No need."

"You don't trust me," Flip said, adding a curse for good measure.

Even through his own physical pain, Jason recognized the hurt in Flip's voice. He recognized it because Flip sounded like Jason had, as a teenager. Gruff, tough, but a mess of pain inside.

"I trust you," Jason said. "And...yeah. You're right. You're all right. Could somebody get me a glass of water?" He reached for the small container of pills in his shirt pocket, but when he pulled them out, he dropped them.

Titan picked up the small container after a couple of tries and dropped it into his hand.

"That's cool!" Ethan said.

"Dude. He slobbered all over it," Flip added.

It was true. Jason wiped the container on his jeans and said "Good" to Titan, who couldn't help the fact that he was a drool machine.

The long-haired veteran had wheeled to the refrigerator and now held out a bottle of cold water to Jason. "Name's Ralph," he said. "Want me to open it?"

"Please." Might as well let these men know how incapable he was.

Not that he had much choice in the matter.

"That a permanent condition you've got, boy?" the ball-cap guy—Freddy—asked.

"Yes, but the pain comes and goes." He needed to get home and lie down on a heating pad. He took the water and popped a couple of pain pills. He swallowed, then looked at Flip. "Now you have to drive me. These things knock me out."

"No problem." Through the boy's careless tone, Jason heard pride that he could actually be a help to someone.

That was something Jason needed to think about—how to make sure the boys did things that genuinely helped others. For now, though, he needed to talk this through before his pills kicked in and made him groggy. "So what do you think would be a good activity our boys could do with the veterans here?" He explained a little about the program, with the boys chipping in some details. He was glad they seemed enthusiastic about the Young Soldiers.

The two older vets looked at each other. "We *have* activities," Ralph said.

"Coming out our ears," Freddy added. "Singing, and current events, and trips to stores." He put his finger to his mouth and made a gagging sound.

The two boys laughed. "I hear that," Flip said. "Ride the Christmas Train. Dig a garden."

"What I'd really like," Freddy said, "is to get outside. I mean, really outside, not in the courtyard here."

"I sure would like to see a trout stream again," Ralph added, a wistful tone in his voice. "Used to work for the Department of Transportation. Drove a mower and a snowplow. Spent my whole life outside, so being in here's like prison."

"Stop feeling sorry for yourself," Freddy said in a

gruff voice that showed his affection for the other man. "At least they let you plow the parking lot when it snows."

"They fixed me up a snowplow with special controls, so I can drive it with my hands," Ralph explained. "They try, but a parking lot's not exactly the wilderness."

"Remember when we sneaked out and drove the snowplow over to clear that cute aide's driveway?" Freddy laughed, and Ralph joined in, high-fiving him.

The two of them didn't seem that different from the teenage boys.

"Could we take you fishing in a van or something? I mean, I've seen the vans around town." Ethan looked pretty interested.

"I could drive," Flip offered. "And I'm guessing *you* know where the trout streams are." He looked at Jason.

"I could figure it out." Jason liked fishing, and periodically checked out a few fishing websites. "I have some limitations on what I can do, physically, but then..." He looked at Freddy, then at Ralph. "Guess we all do."

"We'll have to ask Dr. Green," Ethan said.

"Yeah, well..." That part, Jason wasn't looking forward to. She wouldn't like the way he'd forged ahead on his own and gotten this group of four excited about something that might not even be legitimate or allowable.

Maybe his pain pills were kicking in, breaking down his usual restraints. "We aren't exactly getting along right now."

Flip and Ethan looked at each other.

"A gentleman doesn't speak harshly to a lady," Ethan said.

"And if you want to argue or break up with her, don't do it by text. Talk to her in person." Flip laughed and fist-bumped his friend.

"We're not… Whatever." Somehow, the boys had picked up on the uncomfortable on-again, off-again vibe between him and Ashley.

"Sounds like a story," Ralph said, chuckling.

It was true that he needed to discuss the potential outing with Ashley. He couldn't very well take the boys and veterans anywhere without having Ashley in on it. She'd probably want to join in if she okayed it.

He pictured Ashley in a fishing vest and waders. Surprisingly, it wasn't a bad image. She'd probably do it. She did everything—related to the school and the kids, at least—full strength.

"And be honest about what you're feeling," Flip said.

"Stop throwing my words back at me," he mock scolded. But what Flip said was true.

He needed to tell Ashley about this meeting, but also about the phone call he'd made before Christopher had gotten behind the wheel on that fateful day.

It was going to be hard, and it might well be the end of any relationship they could have, but things weren't going well anyway. Being up-front—while still treating her with good manners—was the way he had to go. He felt a deep certainty inside himself.

And as the boys helped him to his feet, as he shook hands with the older men and promised to be in touch, he realized that he'd thought he was going to help the boys and the elders, but they'd ended up helping him instead.

Wednesday evening, Ashley knocked on Jason's door.

She'd gone back and forth with herself about whether to do it, and as a result of her dithering, it was eight in the evening. She was overstepping her bounds as a neighbor and a boss.

But they needed to have it out about the Young Soldiers program. She hadn't liked the way things had gone at the nursing home last Sunday. And then they'd both gotten busy and hadn't spoken since. Now it was the Wednesday before Christmas vacation. They needed to pin things down.

Was he going to be able to work with her?

Thomas Wilkins, aka the Captain, was coming to the all-school Christmas party tomorrow to say a few words, and he'd want a full report. They needed to hash out their differences now, not in front of him.

Jason opened the door, looking rumpled and sleepy, his flannel shirt untucked, his feet bare, a heavy, end-of-day stubble on his face.

Ashley's mouth went dry. Did he have to be so bad-boy gorgeous? "Uh, hi. I'm sorry—did I wake you?"

"Just about." He yawned. "I was reading and dozing. Come on in."

He seemed more relaxed than he'd been around her lately, and his mood was way too appealing. "I'm sorry to bother you in the evening, but there's something we need to talk about. Work-related," she added hastily so he wouldn't get the wrong idea. "Do you have a few minutes?"

"Sure." He gestured her to the shabby love seat that was in front of the fire and took the equally shabby chair opposite. Clearly, that was where he'd been sitting. There was a thriller, facedown, on the ottoman, and she'd caught a glimpse of a heating pad on the chair-back behind him.

Titan flopped down beside Jason's chair, back end, then front end, bang-bang.

"He rocks the house." She felt a brief flash of longing. Wouldn't it be nice to share the comfort of an evening in front of the fire, reading together?

She pushed that thought aside and got down to business. "Things have been a little awkward between us and we haven't been communicating. We need to catch up, because the Captain's coming tomorrow. He'll want to know how the Young Soldiers program is going."

"Sure. But first, can I get you something to drink? Tea? A soda?"

"Tea sounds nice."

Once he'd disappeared into the kitchen, Ashley extended a hand to Titan. He lifted his huge head and sniffed her hand, then stood and lumbered closer. She pulled back her hand and crossed her arms in front of herself. She wasn't scared he would hurt her, not exactly, but he was just so *big*.

When the dog leaned against her legs, she had to smile at the bid for affection. She ran her hand from his head down his burly body, lightly. When she pulled her hand back, he looked at her with his expressive eyes and nudged at her. His wrinkled face and saggy jowls made her smile.

"You like attention, don't you, boy?" She scratched him behind his short ears as she'd seen Jason do, and he sank to the floor in front of her, slowly, landing on her feet. "I'll never get cold when you're around."

Jason came in carrying two mugs of tea. "Uh-oh, you're talking to him. I do that, too, all the time."

He set one of the mugs on the table beside her, then

sat across from her. Titan watched him, but didn't move from his position on Ashley's feet.

"Is he bothering you? He can get kind of heavy."

"I like it." To her own surprise, it was true.

She also was surprised to find that Jason was a good host. The chairs were set up comfortably, tables beside each one to hold a book or a drink. He'd been quick to welcome her in, and he had drinks to offer. It was more than a lot of single guys would do. Come to think of it, she'd heard people over here a few times recently. He'd had Dev and Emily over for dinner, she knew, and last Sunday afternoon, she'd seen several trucks and heard a lot of male laughter, along with some shouting and cheering and the sound of a football game on TV.

Ashley didn't often have friends over; for some reason, it just didn't occur to her. But being here in Jason's home made her want to be more hospitable herself.

"So what's going on?" he asked, breaking into her thoughts.

She'd been daydreaming, stroking Titan's head, but it was time to get down to business. This wasn't a social call. "The boys said you were making a plan with the veterans at the nursing home. I feel like I should know about that."

"Yeah." He rubbed the back of his neck. "I'm sorry. I meant to tell you sooner. It just kind of happened."

"Did it?" She raised an eyebrow. "I saw you go off with the boys and a couple of the vets, when we were at the nursing home."

"I should have included you," he said immediately. "I'm sorry. It's not an excuse, but I had a pain episode."

"I'm sorry that happened," she said, and decided to

push the issue. "You were short with me before that, though."

"Uh, yeah." He sipped tea. "I…well…"

She waited.

"I wanted to tell you something about Christopher," he said unexpectedly. He set down his tea and she noticed his hand was shaking a little. Was that an effect of his disability, or was he that nervous?

"If that's why things are awkward between us, I guess we should clear the air."

"But now might not be the time, if we need to focus on the Young Soldiers." His words came rapidly. Clearly, he wasn't keen to dive into the subject, even though he'd brought it up himself.

Mixed feelings. She got that. She wasn't all that eager to talk about it herself. "Tell me your plans with the veterans. The boys said something about an outdoor trip. How does that fit in with our goal of getting boys interested in the military?"

"I was thinking about that." Now that the subject of Christopher was temporarily tabled, he seemed more relaxed again. "We'd initially thought it would be more appealing for the boys to be around younger veterans, and I still think we should keep that focus. But I noticed Flip and Ethan really connected with the older men. Almost the way grandparents can get along with teens better than their parents at times."

"That makes sense," she said slowly. "Some of our boys have been raised with grandparents. Others don't know any extended family at all. Either way, mixing the generations could be positive generally."

"But careerwise? Honestly, I'm not sure. The vets we were talking to are Vietnam era. The returning veterans weren't treated well. They can be negative about their experiences."

"Did the men you talked with seem to be that way?"

He shook his head. "No. Nor were they all rah-rah about it. They seemed to have a pretty balanced view, from what I could gather."

"Like you do?"

"In fact, yeah." He sat back in his chair, looking into the fire. "I loved my years in the service, but anyone who looks at me can see that I'm not the same man I was before."

"You have a lot of pain." She wasn't asking a question; she'd seen it firsthand.

"I do. More so at some times than others." He blew out a breath and looked at her. "I don't regret my years in the army, but I would want to be up-front with anyone who enlists. The possible downside is a lot worse than this." He gestured at his own body.

"That's true." She'd had a couple of high school classmates who'd lost their lives serving their country. "And, of course, we want the boys to consider the career option, but not without being aware of the possible cost."

"I feel like those older guys at the home could do that."

"Okay, then." She nodded quickly. "Let's go forward with it. Just keep me in the loop."

"Do you want to come search out fishing holes with us?" he asked. "I mean, I'm sorry I didn't invite you before. The boys and I went once, and then the weather got too bad for exploring. I didn't mean to exclude you."

She quirked an eyebrow. "Didn't you?"

"I *shouldn't* have excluded you, put it that way."

She nodded. "You're forgiven." And now, in the

warm glow of the fire, she hated to break the new sense of accord, but she figured this was the time, if there was a time. “You said you wanted to tell me something about Christopher, but I have something to tell you, too.”

He jerked his head up. “Okay.”

“You might not like me too well after hearing this,” she said. “When Christopher and I were driving, that last time, I…well, I think I caused the accident.”

“What do you mean?”

She sucked in a breath. *Say it now.* “I told Chris some news that upset him a whole lot. I…I told him I was pregnant.”

Jason didn’t speak, and she sneaked a glance at him. His eyes had crinkled with concern. “I didn’t know. Is that…? Oh wow. Is that when your miscarriage happened?”

She nodded and took a deep breath. She needed to say it all, whatever the consequences. “I… Well, he didn’t want us to have a baby, and I did. It was a constant argument between us. I should never have chosen to tell him then, when he was driving. And when he was in such a bad mood. I don’t know why he was in such a bad mood.”

“I do know,” he said slowly.

“You what?”

“I know why he was in a bad mood.” Jason leaned forward, elbows on knees, hands clasped loosely in front of him. “I’d called him just before the two of you left on that trip. I told him… I told him not to hurt you. I was overseas, but I’d heard from Mom that you were going out into the wilderness, Ashley. I just had this terrible feeling he was going to do something to you, and I couldn’t handle it. I called and sort of…threatened him.”

“Whoa.” She stared at him. “So that’s why he thought—” She broke off.

Jason had been staring at the floor, but now he looked up at her, his eyes burning. "Why he thought what?"

"Why he thought the baby was yours." She was reeling, processing it all. "You'd been home for a weekend, and he was paranoid enough to think you and I had hooked up. He said some bizarre things, about how he knew you and I were involved, and how the baby wasn't his." She stared at the floor. "It was the wrong time to get pregnant, and the wrong time to tell him about it. But I wasn't thinking straight, Jason. I wanted so badly to have a baby. Wanted it more than I loved him, wanted it more than I loved God. I made being pregnant an idol, and I was punished."

"You lost your baby."

She nodded. "And my husband. Christopher and I had terrible problems, and I was starting to doubt that the marriage would last. Starting to think I couldn't stay, but I did love him in a lot of ways." She stared down. "So you see, that's why I blame myself. Only now…" She frowned at him. "I wish you hadn't picked that time to call him and tell him not to hurt me. If you hadn't done that…"

"He might not have gotten so angry. But if you hadn't told him you were pregnant—"

"I had to tell him. He was going to find out anyway, and the truth is, I thought I'd be safer in the car than once we'd arrived at the cabin we'd rented, way out in the mountains." She'd had terrifying visions of him killing her and leaving her there, only to be found in the spring.

And once she'd known she was pregnant, her determination to survive had skyrocketed. She'd had to protect her baby.

Only she hadn't. She'd been foolish in how she'd handled everything with her hypersensitive husband. In effect, she'd caused his death. "It was a boy," she said, and her voice broke.

"A… Oh man, Ashley. I'm sorry."

"Me, too." She was angry at him. She was angrier at herself. And she was angry at God. "I can't forgive myself, and to be honest, now that I know your role in it all, I can't forgive you, either."

She stood, feeling like a very, very old woman. "I need to go home," she croaked.

Titan stood when she did, and Jason pushed himself out of his chair, his face as bleak as she felt. "We'll make it through tomorrow," she said. "And then you can go off for your break, and we can both cool off. See where we stand."

"I'm not going home," he said. "Mom and Trent are going on a cruise. I'm staying here. I promised Flip and Ethan we could do some special projects in the shop, since they're both staying."

She narrowed her eyes. "I promised them I'd stay, too."

He threw up his hands. "Great. So we're staying together."

"I'm not any happier about it than you are," she said, and left before they could say more hurtful things to each other.

Chapter Thirteen

As the boys rushed into the cafeteria at the end of the school day on Thursday, caring and love pierced the gloom that had surrounded Jason all day.

Jason was where he was meant to be. He'd questioned that last night. Had God made a mistake, directing him to this job, this life?

But after spending time on his knees, he'd realized that, no, God didn't make mistakes. Jason was helping kids in a way that made full use of his skills and his background. He was in the center of God's will.

Knowing that helped assuage the pain from last night's conversation with Ashley.

The meeting with the Captain that she'd mentioned had never taken place, which might be good news. Jason didn't know if he could sit in a room with Ashley and pretend professional detachment.

A few words emerged from the chaotic noise around him.

"Merry Christmas!"

"School's out!"

"We're do-o-o-ne!"

Boys raced or shuffled around, depending on their ages. Their voices were loud, excited. And why not? They'd just finished the last day of school before break. Now was the all-school Christmas party, and then a special Christmas dinner that was already cooking, making the whole cafeteria smell like turkey and sweet potato casserole and pie.

Tomorrow, parents would arrive to take the boys home for a two-week holiday.

Ashley had her hands full trying to keep the wildly excited students safe as they visited the food tables and located the single gift the school was giving to each of them, which had been hidden treasure-hunt style all around the room.

Jason knew he should be helping her as other staff members were. Instead, he put a hand on Titan's head and watched the scene unfold.

"Okay, okay," Ashley called through the microphone. "If you have your gift, come into the center of the room and sit down. We're all going to open them together."

"Aww, I know what it is," Ricky complained as he ran by. He'd been promoted from a cast to a walking boot, but as far as Jason had seen, he rarely slowed to a walk.

"We all know, dude," an older boy told him.

"Ready, set, rip!"

Everyone ripped into their packages—a book for each boy. Despite a few groans, most of the boys seemed happy as they looked over the gifts and showed each other what they'd gotten.

Jason had heard a little about the process, had even been pulled into it to help choose shop-related books for a couple of the boys who were really into his class. Every book had been carefully selected according to the boys' interests, from motorcycles to politics to manga. A few of the boys, including Flip, actually opened the books and started to read.

Jason strolled around with Titan, talking to boys and staff, finding out about their holiday plans, wishing them a merry Christmas. The only person he avoided was Ashley.

Ashley. Just thinking of her, watching her lively leadership in front of the room, seeing a little edge of tension underneath her smile as she walked around talking and laughing—all of it sent a wash of despair over him.

Her revelations had shocked him, made him angry. But no angrier than he was at himself.

Christopher would always stand between them, even in death. It just wouldn't be possible for them, as a couple, to get past that. And more and more, Jason realized what a loss that was.

He'd come to truly care, beyond the protectiveness he'd always felt toward her, the physical attraction he'd kept under wraps. Now he appreciated her strengths, her talents, the warm way she interacted with kids and staff alike.

It made the loss of her that much keener.

Jason made an effort to push thoughts of Ashley out of his mind. He needed to focus on what really mattered here, what he could do to support the school and the boys.

Ethan and Flip sat a little off to the side, Flip still paging through his new book, Ethan gloomily watching the party.

Jason slid into a chair at their table and instructed Titan to lie down. "You guys doing okay?"

"Yeah." Flip looked up briefly and then returned to examining his new book.

"Sure," Ethan said, "considering I'll be spending the next two weeks the same place I always do."

A hint of an idea started to form in Jason's mind. A way he could make things better for the two boys who couldn't go home—Ethan because his parents were overseas, and Flip because he and his parents had had a huge fight and everyone had agreed he'd be better off spending the vacation at Bright Tomorrows.

A couple of shouts from behind them made them all turn. Ricky was in the process of climbing up onto a chair set on top of a table. Langston Murray was beside him, trying without success to hold the chair steady.

Jason rose as fast as he could, but Flip and Ethan were ahead of him. They ran to the boy, who was now teetering on top of the chair, probably thrown off balance by his walking boot. "Dude! Hang on!" Flip climbed up and caught Ricky as he fell, steadied by Ethan. He swung Ricky down and set him on his feet. "Be careful, or you'll get in trouble before your parents come."

Jason stood by, Titan beside him, watching the boys handle it themselves. He was proud of them. Should he implement the idea he'd just had, about asking if the boys could come stay at his place?

No, because that meant he'd have to talk to *her*.

He looked around and saw that Ashley and Hayley were off at a corner table now, talking intently. Jason didn't want to horn in on that, so he focused on the boys, trying, along with the other staffers, to keep their excitement under control and keep everyone occupied.

Some of the boys were getting rowdier now, and Jason headed over to them, Titan at his side. He didn't want to lay down the law, but he also didn't want anyone to get hurt.

Halfway there, he spotted the Captain, standing in the doorway of the cafeteria with his ramrod-straight posture. He was talking to Mrs. Henry, looking angry. Mrs. Henry seemed to be trying to calm him down.

It wasn't working.

Uh-oh. Ashley was still deep in conversation with Hayley, and the boys were getting louder.

An internal debate arose within him. Should he greet the Captain and explain things, or go warn Ashley?

Before he could decide, Ashley and Hayley both climbed up on the stage, laughing. "Everyone! Pipe down. You're killing our ears!"

"And to kill your ears more, we're going to lead you in some Christmas carols!" Hayley chimed in.

Hayley dialed up something on her phone, and the room was filled with the sounds of "Deck the Halls."

Both of them sang into the microphone. When only a few boys joined in, Ashley jumped down and started circulating, speaking to staff members, who in turn started corralling the boys and getting them to sing.

Jason sighed with relief. Ashley had it all under control.

She headed back up to the stage and Jason made his way over to the Captain, who was frowning.

"Not a very orderly party," he said.

"Yeah. The boys are pretty excited about the last day of school," Jason said, keeping his voice mild and calming.

"I'd like to speak to you and Ashley." The Captain's voice was serious. "Could you get her?"

"Sure." He'd been avoiding her, but a direct order made it so he had no choice, and he found he didn't actually mind too much. He and Titan wove through the boys until they reached the base of the stage. Jason beckoned to Ashley.

She came over immediately and knelt. She was pretty and lean and lithe, and his whole heart hurt with wanting a closeness they couldn't have.

"The Captain wants to speak with us," he said and gestured to the doorway.

"Uh-oh. Sure." She stood, spoke to Hayley, and then beckoned another teacher to the stage and spoke to him briefly, too, apparently asking him to help Hayley lead the singing.

Then she hurried down, and she and Jason walked toward the Captain. This time, the boys moved out of their way. They seemed to sense that Ashley and Jason were on their side, and the Captain, maybe, wasn't.

By the time they reached the doorway, the Captain was gone. But Jason heard a deep raised voice and winced, then turned to where the Captain seemed to be lecturing a small group of boys.

"Intercept?" she asked Jason, raising an eyebrow.

"Let's." They walked over and, when the Captain took a breath, Ashley spoke in a respectful tone. "We're ready to meet with you."

"About time." He glared at them, then at the boys. "You young men, I expect better from you."

Talk about putting a damper on a festive mood.

"Where can we meet?" the Captain barked at Ashley.

"Actually, I'd like to stay here to keep an eye on things," she said. "Or we can wait until the party ends."

The Captain made an irritated gesture. "I'm a busy man. I intended to get here earlier but was held up. And I can't stay long."

"Then let's talk over here." Ashley led the way to

the quietest corner of the cafeteria, which wasn't particularly quiet.

"Things are bad," the Captain said, still standing. "I talked to Marketing, and inquiries aren't any higher than last year. I don't know what you two are doing with the military program, but it's not effective."

"We've only been working on it for six weeks," Ashley said. "You can't expect an initiative to bear fruit that quickly."

"I can, and I do," he said.

Time for Jason to jump in. "We've done a Veterans Day activity, a movie night, and we're planning activities with some older veterans," he said. "Interest in the program is a lot higher than we expected. We have thirty boys signed up."

The Captain raised his hands, palms up. "Fine, but where's the publicity to prospective students and their parents?"

"Actually, we've started sending—"

Some kind of lightweight missile—it looked like a balled-up piece of wrapping paper—hit the Captain in the back of the head.

Ashley marched over to a nearby group of boys and started lecturing them, hotly. Jason made a move to pick up the item and stumbled a little. He steadied himself on Titan, who then picked up the item and deposited it, slightly drool-covered, in Jason's hand.

Sure enough, a wrapping-paper wad.

"I'm sorry for that," Jason said quickly, concerned about the Captain's increasingly red face.

Ashley returned, breathless. "They'll be punished. I apologize for their behavior, sir."

The Captain glared at them both. "I wouldn't be surprised if this is the last Christmas party you'll have at this place. Not only is it out of control, but if you two don't step up your game, this place could go under." He spun and marched out of the cafeteria.

Jason looked at Ashley's bleak face and knew that his own expression was similar. The sad thing was, they couldn't even comfort each other.

On Sunday night, Ashley stood in the church's refreshment hut with Hayley, handing out hot cider and doughnuts to visitors who'd come for the Live Nativity.

She hadn't wanted to come down to town. After the depressing talk with the Captain that had followed the depressing evening with Jason, she'd felt like curling up under her blankets and not getting up until the New Year.

Of course, she'd fulfilled her responsibilities. She'd seen the boys off, talked to parents, helped with issues, wished the staff a merry Christmas. Once everyone was gone, except for the few boys whose families were delayed or who were staying over the break, along with the house parents who were supervising them, she'd gone into an emotional slump.

After she'd missed church this morning, though, Hayley had come over and basically dragged her out. "You need to come keep me company with refreshment duty at the Live Nativity," she said. "I'm leaving tomorrow, and this is our last chance to talk and wish each other a happy holiday. Plus, I have a gift for you."

Ashley had a gift for Hayley, too, and it wouldn't be right to wait until after the holidays to give it to her. Besides, she wasn't doing herself any good by wallowing in despair.

When everything else looked bad—which it did,

given the state of the school and of her relationship with Jason—that was the time to fully rely on God.

The night was frosty cold. And despite the space heater behind them and the bonfire out in the churchyard, both Ashley and Hayley were bundled in winter coats. The Live Nativity actors were doubled up, so that each group was only out for an hour and then could take a break. As the shift changed, they kept busy serving warm drinks and food for the actors as well as the audience members.

Once that rush was over and the second performance began, Pastor Nate stopped by to thank them. "You're both beyond the call of duty, when you should be on your Christmas break," he said. "We appreciate you."

To Ashley, it seemed like his eyes lingered on Hayley, but Hayley got very busy wiping up spills and restocking cups.

"It's no problem," Ashley said. "We're not as busy as you must be during the Christmas season."

"My work is a joy," he said. "Will I see you at the Christmas Eve service?"

"Not me," Hayley said quickly. "I'll be in Arizona, getting warm."

"Nice," he said, though he looked a little disappointed. "How about you, Ashley?"

"I'll be here. I'll see you then."

As the pastor walked away, she wondered whether Jason would attend services on Christmas Eve. If things were different, she'd have loved to go with him.

Hayley was watching the pastor disappear, her expression moody.

"He really likes you," Ashley said.

"Not my type," Hayley said quickly.

"Really? What's not to like about a pastor, especially a good-looking, kind, age-appropriate one like Nate?"

Hayley made a disgusted sound. "You don't want to know. Now, what's going on with you and Jason?"

Ashley supposed the change of subject was fair. "It's over," she said. "If it ever even started."

"Really? Why's that?"

Let me count the reasons. "He did something that contributed to my car accident with Christopher."

Hayley narrowed her eyes. "Didn't you as well?"

"I did," Ashley admitted. "But—"

"And wasn't it all really Christopher's fault?" Hayley interrupted.

"I don't know!" Ashley raised her hands, palms up, feeling frustrated. "I just know that it seems like Christopher is always there between us, and he always will be. Who gets together with their dead husband's brother, anyway?"

"Um, I kinda think that's in the Bible," Hayley said. "But regardless, aren't you selling yourself short, cutting yourself off from an amazing chance for happiness?"

Ashley scanned the area for customers. Seeing none, she leaned back against the front counter. "I just have to get over him."

"Are you sure?"

"Yes! Sadly, yes."

"I wish I could stay and be with you through it," Hayley said. "I always stay, but the chance to go with my aunt to Arizona, the warm weather…"

"And you need to get away," Ashley said firmly. "I'm happy for you."

"I worry about the boys who are staying at the school,"

Hayley said, frowning. "Normally, I'm there to cook special food for anyone who stays, but without me—"

"Relax," Ashley said. "The house parents will take care of it."

"No, they won't." The deep voice behind her danced along Ashley's nerve endings.

Jason.

She turned, and there he was. He was dressed in work clothes, appropriate since he'd been hauling materials for the show; indeed, he'd built the shed they were standing in as well as the stable and manger for the Nativity.

Just being in his presence heated her face and warmed her chest, despite the frigid air.

"That's what I came to talk to you about," he said to Ashley. "Mr. and Mrs. Williams, the house parents who usually stay during breaks, just tracked me down and let me know that they can't stay after all. Something about their daughter needing help with her kids."

"Oh no!" Could anything else go wrong with this day, this season?

"Mrs. Williams said she'd been leaving messages on your phone but couldn't get through. She asked if I could let you know."

Ashley pulled out her phone, which she'd muted, and saw that, indeed, there were several notifications. A quick skim confirmed what Jason had just said.

"I'll stay back," Hayley said quickly. "I can't leave you to deal with them alone. And there's nobody else staying through break, is there?"

"I am," Jason said. "And listen, Ashley, I was thinking this even before the Williamses had their change of plans. What if the boys who are staying over the break come to my place for the two weeks? It would give them a change of pace and a homelike environment. I could cook for them, even decorate a little."

The generosity of the offer almost made Ashley's jaw drop. "You'd do that?"

"I'd enjoy it, actually. I know you'd probably have to get an okay from the parents involved, but it's just Ethan, Flip and, temporarily, Ricky."

"Ricky's staying?" Hayley's eyes widened. "One man isn't enough to handle that kid."

"Just for a couple of days," Ashley said faintly. "His parents are missionaries, and they were delayed in their return trip home." She looked at Jason. "I'm sure the parents would agree, and that would be a wonderful solution, but a lot of work for you."

He shrugged. "Not a problem. Let me know if the parents have any issues with it. Otherwise, I'll start making up the spare beds."

As he walked away, Ashley watched him, almost breathless with amazement over who he was, his kindness, his generosity. It was just more information about what she was giving up in him.

Maybe it was the woodsmoke that made her eyes water.

He turned back. "Oh—and, Ashley," he said, "you don't have to stay, you know. I can handle the boys."

The words stabbed her like sharp knives. He didn't want her around. "It…it's fine. I'll stay," she said.

Because the truth was, she had nowhere else to go.

Chapter Fourteen

Jason woke up Monday morning to sunny blue skies, a prediction of snow on the way and a huge heap of Christmas decorations on his porch.

Plus three sleeping boys upstairs.

Flip and Ethan had been thrilled to escape the cottage where they usually lived and to do a bachelor vacation with Jason.

Ricky was another story. His parents' delay had upset him and he'd cried last night at bedtime. Jason had glared at the other boys to make sure they didn't ridicule the younger boy, and he'd brought Ricky some hot chocolate, but that was about the extent of his nurturing skills. Hopefully, Ricky's parents would arrive later today and all would be well.

He threw on a coat and took his coffee cup outside, standing on the porch while Titan did his business. He surveyed the decorations Dev and Emily had dropped off when they'd heard he was hosting the boys. Truth was, he didn't have much experience putting up outdoor lights. He and the boys would have to learn together.

Next door, Ashley came outside dressed in running clothes, her breaths making clouds in the air. She glanced over and jumped a little, obviously startled. "Oh hey!" she said.

Jason's heart hurt just looking at her. Her blond hair stuck out messily from a red-and-white hat, and her wind jacket looked old and comfortable. She wore running tights that fit like a dream.

He swallowed, his mouth dry. "Hey," he croaked out.

"The boys are settled in?"

"Yeah." He was having trouble getting out more than a word at a time.

"Let me know if you need any help."

He wanted to tell her he might, in fact, need help with Ricky, but he was too dumbstruck by how pretty she looked, all casual and messy. "Will do," he said.

She gave a half smile and a wave, then trotted down the steps. Titan ran to her, wagging his tail, and she knelt to pet him, rubbing his ears and sides. She'd come a long way from the woman who'd been afraid of big dogs.

Then she took off jogging, and Jason forced himself to turn back to the house. He whistled to Titan and they headed inside.

No stirring from upstairs, which he was grateful for; it gave him a few minutes to think and plan the day. He'd wanted to help boys; that had been his dream and his plan when he'd finished his degree and taken the job up here. Hosting them for two weeks, though, was a new challenge. He might be in over his head.

Still, that was a good place to be when your other dreams were shattered.

After another cup of coffee and a glance at the weather report, he roused the boys. Fortunately, Hayley had dropped off a homemade coffee cake before she'd left town. The four of them made quick work of it.

"We've got to figure out how to put up outdoor lights," he told them, and showed them the big stack outside.

"Do we have to? It's cold." Ethan stepped back from the window.

"We'll just have to take them down in a week," Flip added.

Ricky looked crestfallen. "But I want to do it!"

"Me, too," Jason said, "and I get two votes, because it's my house."

The two older boys looked at each other and shrugged. "Just tell us what to do," Ethan said.

"I don't *know* what to do. We have to figure it out."

"Don't you know how to do everything? You teach shop." Ricky was rolling on the floor, waving Titan's toy around. Titan grabbed for it, lazily, his big jaws snapping. He caught it and tugged, pulling Ricky effortlessly across the floor.

"I only seem like I know everything because I watch a lot of YouTube videos," Jason said. "Come on. Let's see what we have, and then we'll come back in and figure out what to do with it all."

Half an hour later, they were stringing lights along the front gutter of the house, Ethan alternating with Flip at the top of the ladder. Ricky had been assigned the job of twisting a string of lights along the porch rail on the grounds that it was too dangerous for him to climb a ladder with his walking boot. Jason kept a sharp eye on the proceedings, knowing how Ricky liked to get in trouble.

"Should we decorate Dr. Green's side, too?" Flip called down.

"Uh, sure." He made a snap decision. Ashley had returned from her run before the boys had made it outside, and she'd gone inside and hadn't come back out, even though they were making plenty of noise.

He wondered what she was doing in there. What was she planning to do for Christmas? Normally, he saw her busy at school. She had friends in town. But at holiday time, she had to get a little lonely. He was pretty sure she didn't have siblings, and her parents were gone.

When Christopher had been alive, they'd spent all their holidays either with his family or traveling for his performances.

He realized, for the first time, that Ashley was alone in the world.

He wanted like anything to invite her to come out and partake in the decorating fun. But he knew it would be wisest to keep his distance. Their relationship wasn't going to work that way long-term. He had all the feelings, but every time he and Ashley got close, some painful memory stopped them.

Since it wasn't going to work, it was best not to open that door.

The boys moved the ladder and strung the lights along her side of the house, too. Ricky came over and twisted lights around her porch rail, the effect crooked and uneven, but Jason wasn't going to correct him. The whole point of this was the activity, not perfection.

The boys got loud as they worked. Flip put some music on his phone, but when he heard the questionable lyrics, Jason nixed it. "Christmas music or nothing," he ordered, and all three boys groaned. But Flip found a music station with trendy Christmas music and Jason let him blare it out.

They worked most of the day and, by nightfall, there was a decent display. Multicolored lights outlined the first floor of the house and wrapped around two spruces outside. A row of lit candy canes lined the walkway to the house, and two wire deer raised and lowered their heads. They'd had a little conflict about a big Santa-and-reindeer decoration, which the boys wanted to put on the roof, but Jason saw the potential disaster there and vetoed the idea, softening his refusal by cooking burgers on the outdoor grill, despite the cold.

He sent Ricky over to deliver a burger to Ashley and invite her to come out. She did, as dusk fell, and oohed and aahed over the decorations. Then she turned to head back inside.

"Wait. Did my mom call?" Ricky asked her, and she glanced at Jason before shaking her head.

"Not yet, honey," she said. "I'll let you know as soon as she does, okay?"

"Are you sure you don't want to stay and eat with us?" Jason asked. He told himself he was only being neighborly, but he could tell from Ashley's level gaze that she thought differently.

"Not tonight," she said, "but I'll tell you what. I've been doing some decorating inside. Why don't you men come over tomorrow and help me finish, and I'll make a big lasagna? We can watch cheesy Christmas movies. It's supposed to snow a lot tonight, so there's no chance to really go anywhere."

"Sounds like a good plan." Jason was grateful that she was helping him find things for the boys to do.

And he was grateful for the opportunity to spend some time with Ashley, despite knowing it wasn't the smartest idea.

The snowstorm was bigger than predicted, and by the time Ashley got up and looked outside, the world was covered in white. Cars were barely distinguishable mounds, and the road looked the same as the yard and fields, all thickly blanketed with snow.

True to Colorado form, the sky was already blue, though according to her phone, the temperature was cold enough that even with sunshine, the snow wouldn't be melting today.

Ashley didn't mind at all—not today, when she had nowhere to be. She climbed back into bed and picked up her Bible. It was good to have more time than usual to stop and reflect. Necessary, too. She'd been on an emotional roller coaster since the Christmas break had started, and it had a lot to do with the man next door.

Normally, she and Hayley would spend Christmas together, a cozy, relaxed girls' holiday, with cookies and movies and gossip. Today would be different.

She read her Bible, and a devotional, and spent some time ticking off everything she was grateful for, thanking God for health and a warm place to live, a job she loved. As always, her devotional practice grounded her.

She was stuck inside, alone for now, but she'd soon be confronted with a houseful of boys—or at least three boys and a man, which felt like a houseful. She got up, grabbed coffee, turned on Christmas music and started to cook.

Throughout the morning, she heard the sound of shovels scraping and boys yelling and laughing. When she looked out, the two older boys were pulling Ricky on a sled, while Jason and Titan brought up the rear. They disappeared into the trees and she gathered they were going sledding. But when they came back, a Christmas tree was tied to the sled. They were all laughing and soaked, and it was another hour before there was a tap on her door.

All of them wore dry clothes and they were starving. Ashley served up big plates of lasagna and bowls of salad, and garlic bread made from frozen homemade loaves. It was gratifying to see them all eat their fill.

"No dessert," she said, "unless you want to make and decorate cookies yourselves. That's what I'm planning to do this afternoon." She hadn't expected the boys to want to participate in such a domestic activity, but to her surprise, Ricky and Flip jumped on it. Ethan and Jason elected to keep the walkways and porch shoveled off, since it had started to snow again.

In the middle of pulling sheets of sugar cookies out of the oven, Ashley got the call she had hoped she wouldn't get. It was Ricky's mother. "We're not going to make it," the woman said, her voice choked. "Our flight was delayed again, and even if we did make it to Denver, we wouldn't have a vehicle that could get up into the mountains."

"We'll take good care of him," Ashley promised. "Two other boys are spending the vacation at the school, and our new shop teacher has them all staying at his place for the holiday, keeping them busy."

"That's good, but…" The woman was crying. "He's my baby."

"It must be so hard." She sank into a chair. "He's here now, baking cookies. Would you like to talk to him?"

Ricky's shoulders had slumped more and more as she'd talked to his mom. Now he took Ashley's phone and went to the far side of the kitchen, and she saw him slide down to the floor, cross-legged, head bowed.

Jason and Ethan came in the back door, stomping snow off their boots. "Smells good," Ethan said, taking his boots off and slipping past them into the front room toward the sound of a football game on TV.

Jason took his boots off, too, and the sight of him padding over in wool socks warmed something inside Ashley.

"Everything okay?" he asked.

She nodded at Ricky. "His parents can't make it."

"Uh-oh. He was already upset."

"I figured. He seemed a little quieter than usual." She slid another tray of cookies into the oven.

"Kid is bummed." Flip was stirring food coloring into small bowls of white icing with the precision of a chemist. "Cookies will help." As soon as Ricky got off the phone, Flip called to him. "Get over here, kid. We have cookies to decorate."

Ricky wiped his eyes and headed over, with a detour at the sink to wash his hands.

Jason smiled, watching them, and that made Ashley smile, too. "They're good boys," she said.

"And this is good work," he said. He gamely joined in on the cookie decorating.

Later in the afternoon, after the cookie decorating was finished and Jason, Ricky and Flip had disappeared into the living room to watch football, Ethan came in. "Got Ralph and Freddy on a video call," he said. "I'm going to show them our outdoor lights and our food."

"You're a sweet kid." Ashley broke her own rule and put an arm around him, giving him a quick squeeze.

He grinned, letting her do it. Then he turned slowly with the phone camera, showing the veterans the kitchen and the wildly decorated cookies. Ashley assured them that as soon as the weather cleared, they could come up and see for themselves, and get cookies.

"If there are any left," Flip said, coming into the room and stuffing one in his mouth.

Ethan wandered outside to show the lights, and then came back in, the veterans still on the call. "Where's Ricky?" he asked Ashley.

Ashley looked around the kitchen. "I think he's watching TV," she said, and called into the living room, "Hey, Flip, Jason, is Ricky with you?"

"Nope."

"I thought he was in the kitchen." Jason stood and came to the doorway.

"He's not." Ashley's stomach knotted and she hurried through the house, checking the bathrooms and bedrooms. "He's not in the house," she reported back.

"Flip, go check next door. He probably went over to take a nap or something." But Jason's tone indicated worry.

A thorough search of both places yielded nothing. "His boots are gone, and his coat," Ethan noted.

Jason turned on the outdoor lights and looked outside. "It's snowing pretty hard, but there are tracks," he said. "If he's gone out into the storm, we'd better find him before dark."

Ashley looked over his shoulder into the gloom, swallowing hard. Today was the winter solstice, the shortest day of the year. It was almost dark now.

She grabbed her coat and glanced at her phone. There was a text message on the lock screen.

Ashley, this is Ricky's mom. He called and left me a message from someone's phone. He says he's coming down to meet us at the bottom of the hill, but we're still at the airport. Please tell me he's safe with you!

"Hey, what's that?" Ethan pointed to a folded piece of paper on the table.

Ashley opened it and squinted to decipher Ricky's handwriting. "He's gone down to meet his parents," she said, her heart sinking. "On foot. And they won't be there when he gets to the bottom of the hill. If he even makes it."

Chapter Fifteen

Jason insisted that someone had to stay at the house in case Ricky came back there. He wanted it to be Ashley, but she wanted to help search, so Flip agreed to stay and keep circling the house and grounds every few minutes. If there was no word in fifteen minutes, he'd call the police. They'd all stay in touch by cell phone.

Even as he took charge of organizing everyone, Jason was beating himself up. How on earth had he let this happen? He was responsible. Ten minutes ago, he'd been relaxing in the warm house, enjoying the smell of cookies and the sounds of happy kids, popping into the kitchen to grab a soda and chat with Ashley.

He'd been enjoying that more than he should have been.

But now everything had changed. A child was missing and the weather was getting worse, and darkness was falling. If something happened to Ricky, it would be on him.

"I feel awful," Ethan was saying. "He was with me. I should have kept track of him."

"No, I should have," Ashley said.

Jason realized he had to set an example. "We can't get stuck in what-ifs," he said. "Everyone use your skills. Think what you can do to help find him."

"I'm filming this to get the word out on social media," Ethan said.

Jason hadn't expected that answer, but it wasn't a bad idea. "Good. Do that. Ashley, you know him best. What would he be thinking and where would he go?"

Meanwhile, as she talked, thinking aloud, he was using the tracking skills he'd learned in the military to lead all of them along the boy's path, despite the wind and weather that made progress slow. The snow sent sharp ice pellets against his face and the deep drifts made him stagger. More than once, he had to lean on Titan, who was having trouble of his own getting through the snow.

It was an hour before they got halfway down the mountain road, looking in all directions and yelling until they were hoarse.

A motor engine sounded and a light up ahead pierced the darkness. "It's a plow!" someone said.

"I can't believe they'd plow us out already," Ashley said. "It usually takes a day. Did someone call the county, or roadside assistance?"

"It's not a regular plow," Ethan said, filming it. "It's..."

Ashley squinted through the darkness. "It's Ralph and Freddy!" she cried at the same time Jason recognized the two elders, bundled against the snow, high atop an ancient-looking snowplow.

"Came to help," Ralph called from the plow's front seat.

"We were still on the call when the child came up missing." Freddy climbed down.

Ralph stayed in the driver's seat. "Tell me where you think the boy might be," he said, "and I'll plow you a path."

Jason thought he saw a track and leaned over, looking at it. At the same moment, Freddy knelt to study the snow. They looked at each other, and Freddy nodded. "Over this way—but careful," he called to Ralph, and the man slowly plowed a path while the rest of them guided him and checked the snowdrifts all around.

Titan let out a bark and lifted his head.

There was a flash of a red coat, and then they were all running toward it, hearing the welcome sound of Ricky's crying.

Ashley wrapped her arms around the boy, hugging him, crying herself. "You scared us, kiddo. Are you all right?"

"I'm cold," Ricky said through chattering teeth.

"Got blankets and foot warmers in the plow," Freddy said. "How would you like a ride back home?"

"On a plow? Yeah!" Ricky tugged out of Ashley's arms and was soon tucked in between the two veterans, chugging up the road toward the house.

There were no coincidences, Jason reflected as he, Titan, Ethan and Ashley made their way up the hill behind the plow. Just a lot of human mistakes.

Jason had let a child get lost today. But he'd also helped find him.

Ashley slipped an arm around him. "I can't believe how that worked out. Praise God, he's safe."

"Praise God is right." He tugged her to his side, helping her through the snow as best he could, though they were really holding each other up. "You know, we both messed up to some degree today, just like we did with Christopher. But that's life. We can be forgiven for our mistakes, both of us."

She didn't answer, but she tightened her arm around him in a way that showed she'd heard what he was saying.

Ethan jogged ahead to catch video of the snowplow with the vets and Ricky atop it. As for Jason, he relished the feeling of Ashley beside him. He wondered why he'd been so mad and focused on the past when life was short. "This is worth fighting for," he said, and then he wasn't sure if he'd said it aloud or not.

He'd meant it, though. Meant it with all his heart.

Christmas Day dawned sunny and bright. The roads were plowed and mostly dry, and it was hard to remember how scared and trapped they'd felt just four days ago. But Ashley could never forget what God had done for them that night, what He was still doing.

Ashley and Jason were working together now without awkwardness, united in their desire to make a Christmas for the boys. After the scare with Ricky, clinging to guilt and fear just seemed wrong. Life was short and God was good.

There was a knock on the door. When she wiped her hands and went to answer it, Ashley was shocked to see her in-laws. Shocked, too, at how happy she was to see them. She opened her arms and hugged Trent and then, more gently, Marsha.

"We couldn't stay away," Marsha said. "Jason told us he couldn't come, and...well, I realized some things. I should have been inviting you to family holidays all this time. I'm sorry I didn't."

It was clearly a prepared speech, but not in a bad way.

"Come inside," Ashley said. "I'm working on dinner, and Jason and the boys are next door."

Mr. Green went next door with the boys while Ashley and Jason's mother cooked; a weird but good thing. The woman seemed stronger than she had at Thanksgiving, though she still showed evidence of tiredness, like when she took the celery and onions she was chopping to the table and sat to do the work.

They chatted about the recent storm, the boys, and a couple of relatives Ashley knew slightly, who lived back East. Then Marsha pushed her work aside and leaned forward.

"I feel like I need to explain the reason I've been unfriendly to you," she said.

"No, no, I understand. We've all gone through such a hard time." She heard the front door opening, the boys coming in, the TV being turned on and then down.

"I've felt so guilty about Christopher's death," Marsha continued. "I've been speaking with a counselor, because of my illness and...well, everything that's happened. My own guilt is part of what's come out."

Ashley turned down the stove burners and sat beside Marsha. "I've felt guilty, too," she said. "Horribly so, and I still do." And it was time to be open about everything. If Marsha could do it, so could she.

Gently, carefully, she explained about her pregnancy and her poor timing in relaying the news to Christopher.

Behind them, a throat cleared. Jason came into the kitchen. "I couldn't help overhearing. You may both feel guilty, but most of the fault lies with me." He sat kitty-corner from his mother and took her hand. "You see, I called Chris right before he and Ashley left on that last car ride. I confronted him about some things, and it didn't sit well. That's why he was in such an awful mood when they started off."

Marsha bit her lip, clearly trying to hold back tears. She kept hold of Jason's hand and reached out to grasp Ashley's as well.

"It may not have been the best idea to speak with him that way," Ashley said to Jason, "but you did it from good intentions, to keep him from making a horrible mistake."

He met her eyes for a long moment and then looked down at the table. "I'll never forgive myself for my role in taking his life and…" He swallowed. "And the life of your unborn child."

Mrs. Green sat straighter. "No. You children may have made some mistakes, but I'm by far the most at fault. I should have raised Christopher differently. He was spoiled, and never heard the word *no*, and it made him selfish and entitled." She looked at Jason. "It wasn't fair to you. I was never fair to you, and I'm sorry."

"Water under the bridge, Mom." He looked at her, tenderness and compassion obvious in his eyes. "I made plenty of mistakes growing up. I was a handful."

"You were a wonderful child and you're a wonderful man. I should have paid more attention to that and less to Christopher's special talents. You've done so much more good in the world than he was ever able to do." Marsha's eyes shone with unshed tears. "I was so glad to finally carry a child to term that I indulged him, not realizing it wasn't good for him. Now we're all paying the price."

"We are," Ashley said softly, "but we're fallible humans who make mistakes. Maybe we can't forgive ourselves, but God forgives us."

Marsha studied her face for a long time. "Your faith always was an inspiration to me," she said. "I wish I could feel that way."

"You can, Mom," Jason said. "I'm new at this faith thing, but I get what Ashley said. It's what the Bible teaches."

The woman shook her head. "It's been so long since I've set foot inside a church. I need to go back. Maybe I'd find some peace."

Ashley squeezed her hand. "I hope you will. Look, tomorrow's Sunday. Stay here tonight and come to church with us." She looked up at Jason. "You'll come to church and bring the boys, won't you?"

He met her eyes, held them, and something arced between them. Some spark. "Of course I will."

And as they finished preparing dinner, as they ate a meal with the boys, sharing laughter and a few tears, too, Ashley felt cleansed in the way that only God could cleanse a person.

She was a sinner, but so was everyone else in this fallen world. The beauty was that God's grace could redeem anyone.

Thankfulness and joy swirled through her heart, filling her with love for her difficult former in-laws, these boys in her care and, especially, this man.

On New Year's Eve, Jason strolled through Little Mesa's lit-up downtown with Ashley on one side, Titan on the other, and a small box in his pocket.

Was he really going to propose this soon? It felt like he was jumping the gun. But there was a reason he had a ring already, and now that he had it, he wanted to give it to her and settle things between them, make it permanent.

The knowledge that he loved Ashley had been growing on him ever since he'd come to work at the school, but the time they'd spent together during the holidays had crystallized everything for him. Seeing her love for the boys, her compassion, and her sense of fun, had made him sure she was exactly the woman with whom he'd like to raise a family.

The talk with his mom and Ashley, plus Nate's sermons and his own prayers, had finally convinced him that he could be forgiven for his mistakes. He didn't have to punish himself forever. There was such a thing as grace.

He'd spoken to his mom about it before she and his stepfather had left after Christmas, and she was the one who'd suggested he use her engagement ring from when she'd married his father so long ago. A few days later, he'd driven to Denver to get it. He hoped it didn't seem like he was going cheap or secondhand. The truth was, it was beautiful, classic like Ashley, and Mom had been touched he'd agreed to use it.

He and his mother had had another good talk, and he was committed to spending more time with her in the coming months. Despite their past issues, he was the only son she had left, and he was determined to fulfill his responsibilities. He wanted to love and value her to the best of his ability, to help her face her fight with cancer. Maybe, to give her a reason to want to heal.

Ashley was smiling and waving at people, clearly enjoying the night stroll and the lights. For all her education and her past difficulties, she'd managed to retain a childlike sense of wonder, and he loved that about her.

"Did I tell you Ricky's family made a donation to the school?" she asked. "A nice one. They're grateful for what we did for him over the break, and especially when he was lost."

"I don't suppose it's enough of a donation to ease up the pressure to enroll more students?"

"Unfortunately, no." Her face darkened for a moment and then cleared. "I want to save the school, so much. But all I can do is my best, and I'm doing that. I know you are, too." She leaned closer and gave him the quickest of side hugs. "I appreciate you."

He felt that—the sentiment and the physical closeness—all the way into his bones. He touched the box in his pocket. "Let's walk over this way," he said, moving in the direction of a lit archway with a bench underneath, currently deserted.

It wasn't a social-media-worthy proposal site, but then, Ashley wasn't the type to want a photo-op proposal. Neither was Jason.

"Hey, you two!" It was a family from church whom Jason had met a couple of times. They stood out because their little girl was a wild one; the kind of kid who couldn't cooperate during the children's choir performance, but had to push her way to the front of the group and wave and yell to her family.

"Titan!" she shouted now, running toward the dog.

"Natalie! No!" The father ran and snatched her up just before she reached Titan. "You can't touch a dog without asking. Especially when he's wearing a red vest."

"I want to play with him!" Her lower lip stuck out and she kicked at her father.

"I'm sorry," the mother said, and then reached out for

Natalie. "Come to Mommy, honey. Remember, we're going to get you a puppy if you're good."

"You shouldn't promise her that!" The father frowned.

"It's the only thing that works!" the mother snapped. She carried Natalie over to the arbor where Jason had been headed.

"Sorry, you guys. Happy New Year." The father hurried over to sit with his family.

Oh well.

Jason wished them the best. There were plenty of pretty places in Little Mesa. He could pop the question elsewhere.

They'd just continued walking down the street, Jason scouting for promising private spots, when Hayley rushed up to them. "I'm in trouble, you guys. I've dawdled around and I'm late to the lockup. I don't know if I even want to go."

Jason raised an eyebrow. "You volunteered for that?" The youth group was spending the night together at the church and, to his surprise, Ethan and Flip had been eager to join in.

When they'd dropped the boys off, he'd gotten an insight into why they'd wanted to participate: there were a number of girls planning to stay.

"You should go." Ashley seemed to be fighting a smile. "Pastor Nate will definitely be glad for *your* help."

"Stop it!" Hayley pulled Ashley off to the side and they talked for what seemed to Jason like a very long time.

Finally, Hayley dashed off for the church and Ashley came back to his side.

This time, he was definitely getting her alone, out of

the crowd. He took her mittened hand and urged her toward a not-so-busy area up ahead.

She didn't pull her hand away, but there was a speculative look in her eye. They hadn't done a lot of handholding, maybe that was why. Hopefully, that was about to change.

"Come on over here," he said. "I have something I want to talk to you about."

He was almost to a little gazebo in the park—which was better than the arbor, more private—when there was a shout behind them.

A shout they both recognized.

"What's the Captain doing here?" Now Ashley *did* pull her hand away from his.

"No clue," Jason said, sighing.

"I've been looking for you. I heard you were out here." The man approached them, rubbing his hands together, stamping his feet. "I should've dressed warmer, but I didn't anticipate having to look this hard for you."

"What's going on, sir?" There was a slight undertone of dread in Ashley's voice. A month ago, Jason wouldn't have recognized it, but he knew her so much better now.

"I would never have believed it, but you two did it."

Jason now shared Ashley's worry. "What did we do, sir?"

"Didn't you see that young man's social-media post? The one that went viral?"

"No…" Jason looked at Ashley. "Did you?"

"I'm not on that much social media," she said. The dread was obvious. "What was it about? Whose post, and on what platforms?"

"You're out of touch!" The Captain sounded exuberant. "Even though it's vacation, Mrs. Henry saw it, and then she checked the website. Online applications have been flooding in. Our applications are up sixty percent for next year!"

"What?" Ashley sounded bewildered, as bewildered as Jason felt.

"Look, I'll show you." He pulled out his phone and flipped expertly through various apps, landing on one that seemed to feature mostly videos.

And there they were—Ashley and Jason, running through the snow. Ricky, swept up into Ashley's arms. The veterans driving triumphantly on the plow, Ricky tucked in between them.

There were captions; something about the school and what it meant to boys like Flip, Ethan and Ricky. The ending captured Titan's panting, smiling face.

"All that time Ethan was making videos and I thought he was just fooling around and being annoying...he was doing *this*?" Jason hadn't realized such a sophisticated-looking product was even possible from filming on a phone.

"That went viral?" Ashley asked.

"Yes! On a number of different platforms. It's as good as one of those Christmas movies women can't stop watching. Everyone loves a happy Christmas story." He lifted his hands, palms up. "Including, apparently, boys who need the kinds of services we offer, and their parents." He shook Jason's hand, vigorously, and then Ashley's. "Well done."

"Thank you for letting us know," Ashley said faintly. "And please make sure you tell Ethan how well he did." She frowned. "But how were you in touch with Mrs. Henry?"

The Captain's cheeks reddened—or at least it seemed

that way to Jason. "She's a widow, and I wanted to check on her over the holidays. I know how hard they can be after a loss."

There was the honk of a car horn on a side street. "Thomas! Over here!"

"Happy New Year to both of you," he said, and hurried off toward the unmistakable sound of Mrs. Henry's voice.

"Talk about a happy Christmas story," Jason commented. He'd never have pegged the Captain for falling in love, but it seemed to be the season for second chances.

"That *is* interesting," Ashley said, looking after the man with a bemused expression on her face. And then she turned to Jason, eyes shining. "Oh, Jason, we did it! With God's help, we all saved the school!"

He nodded, treasuring her happiness.

"All of us," she went on. "The vets, Flip and Ethan, you and me. Even Ricky had a role to play. And Titan, when you think about it. And I see God's hand over the whole situation."

"You're right, and I'm happy. Really happy. But..."

This night was not going the way he'd hoped it would. "Look, here's Café Aztec. Let's go inside and have some hot chocolate. If we can find a quiet corner, I do want to have that talk."

Ashley sat in a secluded corner of Café Aztec. Somehow, Jason had gotten them a table by the big fireplace, and its warmth radiated through her. And that was wonderful, but she still felt chilled inside.

What did he want to tell her?

When he'd asked her to keep an eye on Flip and Ethan while he drove down to Denver a few days ago, she'd pushed aside her worry that he might be interviewing for another job. Now she wondered uneasily about his insistence that they needed to talk.

Maybe he'd decided that, having helped to turn things around at the school, he was ready to move on.

The thought of Jason not being there, in the place next door, in the classroom down the hall, hollowed her out inside.

I've fallen in love with him.

She didn't know when it had happened, but there it was. Full-blown love. The kind that made her long to be close to him, that made her happy just to see his face or to take a walk beside him.

If he left, she might not be able to bear it.

The waiter who'd approached did a double take at the sight of Titan. "Sir, no dogs in the… Oh!" He squinted through the dimness. "A service dog?"

"Yes."

"*Lo siento.* Of course, he is welcome, as are you. What would you like to drink?"

"Your hot chocolate has a pretty good reputation, doesn't it?"

The waiter smiled and kissed the tips of his fingers. "It is a beautiful thing."

"I'll have that," Ashley said, deciding instantly, and Jason said, "Make it two."

When they were alone, she looked at Jason and her eyes seemed to blur until he was all she could see. "No matter what you're about to tell me," she said, reaching for his hand and squeezing it, "it's been a wild, wonderful ride."

"It has." He turned his hand over and captured hers. "And I hope it can continue, Ashley."

She could hardly dare to hope. "It can? You'll stay at Bright Tomorrows?"

He tilted his head to one side. "Of course I will, if you'll have me. That was never in question."

"But I thought…when you went to Denver… Never mind." Relief and happiness danced inside her. "I'm so glad. You're a wonderful teacher and role model, and you're so good for the boys. I'm delighted you'll stay."

"Well…thank you. I'm glad you like my work. But, Ashley…there's something more I want to talk about."

Their hot chocolate arrived and Ashley took a nervous sip. Flavor exploded in her mouth: deep, rich chocolate, along with vanilla and cinnamon, and maybe nutmeg. She could tell Jason wanted to be serious about something, but she couldn't let this deliciousness pass without comment. "This is the best hot chocolate I've ever had. Wow!" She took another sip. "Thank you for bringing me here."

"I've always heard Mexican hot chocolate is the best, and now I know that's true." They both sipped again as the sound of jazzy holiday music and people's voices, talking and laughing, surrounded them.

Jason reached across the table and took her hand. His was calloused; the hand of a workingman. She stared at their hands together for a minute and then looked up at his face. *Here it comes, whatever it is.*

"Ashley," he said, "there's not really a subtle way to say this."

"Then don't be subtle."

"Okay." He took a deep breath and then let it out again. "I want to marry you."

"What?" She couldn't process it. He seemed to have said… "Say that again."

"I want to marry you." He held up a hand. "Don't say anything yet. I want you to know why. I love so many things about you. The passion you have for your work and the kids, the way you can have fun despite all the cares on your shoulders."

She couldn't have spoken now if her life depended on it—she was that shocked.

"You forgave my mom despite how awful she was to you. That says a lot about you." He hesitated, then took another deep breath. "I'm not going to deny I think you're gorgeous. That's part of what draws me to you. But it's way deeper than that. You have a strong faith, and that makes me have more faith." He paused, then added, "We could be good together. Really good."

She just stared at him as her feelings spiraled out of control, stunned, and warm, and wonderful.

"I love you, Ashley." He squeezed her hand. "I'd like to keep proving that to you for the rest of our lives."

Now it was her taking deep breaths, trying to retain some kind of rational thought. "But…what about Christopher? Our past? I've felt it as a barrier, not to my heart, but just…just between us."

He nodded seriously. "We're not starting clean, are we? We can't pretend he wasn't part of our lives and isn't part of our history, and I wouldn't want to. But we can move on."

"What about your mom?" Her mind seemed to be coming up with all the reasons this wouldn't work, couldn't be true. "I don't want to upset her, not now."

"She's happy about it. In fact…" He slid out of their booth and, with Titan's help, got to his knees. He reached into his pocket and pulled out a box. "This isn't spur-of-the-moment. I came prepared to propose. So—" he cleared his throat and looked at her with love in his eyes "—will you marry me, Ashley?" He opened the box and held it out.

The beautiful, old-fashioned ring inside was what made it real to her, made it seem possible. Made tears spring to her eyes. "It's gorgeous," she choked out, and looked from the ring to his strong, square-jawed face, a face she'd come to love. "I love it."

"It was Mom's engagement ring from my dad. That's why I drove down into Denver last week, to talk to her about wanting to propose and to shop for a ring. It was Mom who suggested you might like this one."

"It's perfect," she said. "*You're* perfect, Jason, and I can't believe..."

"I'm not perfect." He was still on his knees.

Tears were rolling down her cheeks now. This man... This courageous man who'd served his country and was now putting his energy into serving troubled youths. Who'd been brave in a crisis and fun over the holidays. Who was generous with the boys, sharing what he had.

Who was the most handsome man she'd ever seen.

She couldn't believe that God would give her so much, but then again, that was God. She closed her hand over the ring box. "I love you, Jason Smith," she said, "and I would love to marry you."

He got to his feet with Titan's help and pulled her into his arms. Only dimly did she hear some muted clapping from the other diners.

She was where she wanted to be, forever. In his arms.

Epilogue

Five months later

It was spring cleanup day at Bright Tomorrows Residential Academy, and Ashley did *not* feel well.

Emotionally, she felt great. She was happy, ecstatically happy, since she'd married Jason on Valentine's Day earlier this year. Their marriage was everything she'd ever dreamed of and more. It had seemed perfect in the beginning, but somehow, it got better, deeper, richer every day.

Her stomach was just shaky, that was all.

She was able to fake feeling okay for long enough to get the boys revved up and cleaning, and then she retreated to a quiet bench outside the school's front doors.

"Are you okay?" Hayley asked, coming up to her. "It's not like you to sit down when there's an activity at the school."

"I'm fine, just a little queasy." The reason for it made it impossible not to smile.

Hayley stared, tilted her head to one side. "You're pregnant." It wasn't a question.

"You guessed? How?" They'd told no one, except for Trent and Marsha, last night, after they'd passed the three-month mark and gotten a good report from the obstetrician.

"Nothing else would make you so happy even though you're queasy," Hayley said. "Plus, Jason is walking around today like he's ten feet tall."

It was true: they were both thrilled to be expecting a baby, even though it was soon after the wedding. Although she hadn't expected to conceive so quickly—on her honeymoon, in fact—Ashley was so, so ready to be a mother, and Jason felt the same about fatherhood. Working with young people was what had brought them together, and they both felt it as their mission. Becoming parents would extend that mission—and that joy—exponentially.

Hayley shaded her eyes, looking through the bright sunlight into the school's parking lot. "Is that somebody's parents? Grandparents?"

"I don't think anyone's due today." Ashley squinted, too. "Flip starts basic training in two weeks. His parents are coming, but I'm not sure when."

"Ricky's mom and dad?" Since they'd become benefactors, they'd taken to visiting the school much more frequently.

"No, it's... Oh wow!" Ashley stood. "It's Trent and Marsha!"

She hurried out to greet them. Marsha was visibly weaker than she'd been at the wedding, no doubt the result of some tough cancer treatments, but her smile was huge. "I had to come to congratulate you in person when I heard the news," she said. "I'm thrilled I'm going to be a grandmother."

They hugged long and hard, both of them knowing all the pain that had come before, pain that made this moment bittersweet.

"Now, let's find you two a place to sit. And remember, it's just a short visit," Trent said.

Once they were settled side by side on a couch in the teachers' lounge, Marsha studied her anxiously. "I know it can be a strange time, getting pregnant after losing a baby," she said. "Are you doing okay?"

"I do have some bouts of sadness," she said, surprised her mother-in-law understood that. Then again, the woman had been through it.

"That's normal. It won't change your joy in the new baby, remembering the one you lost."

"Thank you."

They talked a little about the pregnancy and about Marsha's treatments for her cancer, which were going well. "I have every reason to get through this and get strong again," she said. "I want to meet the newest member of the family."

Ashley's throat tightened. Pregnancy emotions. But it was more than that. "I want that, too, so much." She held Marsha's hand and marveled at the healing God had done between them.

The door opened and Jason strode in. "Mom! I heard you were here. Is everything okay?"

"Just paying a short visit. Not to you—to Ashley." She presented her cheek for a kiss. "But you can take me to get a couple of those wonderful cookies from your cafeteria, and then we'll head home."

Trent had followed Jason in. "I'll take you to the cafeteria," he said. "That way I can make sure we get a few extra cookies for the road."

After they'd all hugged and Trent and Marsha had left, Jason sat beside Ashley. "Was that okay?" he asked. "I didn't expect them to show up as soon as we told them."

"It was lovely. How's the cleanup going?"

"It's going well. The mark of a good leader—you've trained everyone to do their job fine without you."

"Good, because I'm planning to take some time off with the baby." But they'd agreed they wanted to stay at Bright Tomorrows. They'd purchased the duplex and the small lot it stood on from the school. As soon as the weather was reliable, they'd start renovations, making it into a single-family home.

A home for their family. Ashley still could barely believe it.

"You sure you don't need anything?" Jason asked, putting an arm around her. "A back rub, maybe?"

"A back rub would be nice, later," she said, stretching and then nestling into his embrace. "But I don't *need* it. All I need is you."

* * * * *

If you enjoyed this K-9 Companions book by Lee Tobin McClain, be sure to pick up her previous contribution to the miniseries, Her Easter Prayer.

And look for more K-9 Companions stories coming from Love Inspired!

Don't miss Lee Tobin McClain's latest full-length romance, The Bluebird Bakery, *available January 2023 from HQN Books!*

Dear Reader,

Thank you for returning with me to the Bright Tomorrows Residential Academy. Ashley was first introduced in *Her Easter Prayer*, and she tugged at my heartstrings. I wanted her to find love. And suddenly there was Jason, a voice from her past, a veteran and a dedicated teacher… the perfect hero for her and for this Colorado-set Christmas story.

Ashley and Jason share a passion for education. That's something that runs in my family, too. My grandparents taught in a two-room schoolhouse in Kentucky, and my mother taught middle school and high school in Ohio. I've been a college professor for many years, and my sister teaches GED students. I'm proud to say that my daughter is on the path to becoming a middle-school teacher herself. So you see, writing about a school makes all the sense in the world for me!

I'd love it if you would join my newsletter so that you can be notified of my new releases. You can also grab a couple of free novellas along the way.

Merry Christmas!
Lee

COMING NEXT MONTH FROM
Love Inspired

SNOWBOUND AMISH CHRISTMAS
Amish of Prince Edward Island • by Jo Ann Brown

Kirsten Petersheim's new life plan involves making a success of her housecleaning business—and doesn't include love. Then her new client Mark Yutzy asks for advice about dealing with his troubled teenage brother. This Christmas she might reconsider a future that involves the handsome farmer.

AN AMISH CHRISTMAS INHERITANCE
by Virginia Wise

When Katie Schwartz inherits her late aunt's farm in Lancaster County, she's eager to run her own business. But widowed single dad Levi Miller owns half the farm and isn't giving up without a fight. When they must unite to save the property from foreclosure, will they discover they share more than an inheritance?

THE MISTLETOE FAVOR
Wyoming Ranchers • by Jill Kemerer

With the holidays approaching, wealthy rancher and new guardian Mac Tolbert enlists coffee shop owner Bridget Renna to hire his withdrawn teenage sister. Fresh from New York, Bridget is doing her best to live independently in Wyoming, but as she bonds with Kaylee and soon Mac, will the truth about her past threaten their growing love?

HER SECRET SON
Sundown Valley • by Linda Goodnight

After discovering injured Nash Corbin on her ranch, Harlow Matheson is surprised at how quickly long-buried feelings begin to resurface. For Nash, spending time with the girl he left behind is the best part of this homecoming. Until he meets the son he never knew existed...

THE CHRISTMAS SWITCH
by Zoey Marie Jackson

Switching places with her twin sister wasn't part of Chanel Houston's holiday plans. Yet with a sibling in need, she can't refuse to help. But as she falls for her sister's next-door neighbor Ryder Frost, his adorable little girl and his rowdy puppy, can she keep the secret?

A NANNY FOR THE RANCHER'S TWINS
by Heidi Main

Cattle rancher Ethan McCaw desperately needs a nanny for his twin daughters. His neighbor Laney Taylor is seeking a contractor to convert her house into a wedding venue. He'll agree to renovate her place if she cares for his girls. Can they take a chance on a future—together?
